P9-DNV-238

"Since we barely know each other, I think we need to allow each other an escape clause."

"What do you mean?" A gamut of perplexing emotions flooded through Tanner. One minute Jordana was talking about being true and how hard her parents had worked at making their marriage work, now she was negotiating an *escape clause?*

"What I mean is we hardly know each other and we're talking about taking a step that people who have known each other for years agonize over. Think about it…what if we get married and we end up being incompatible?"

Honey, you and I are way too compatible. That's what got us into this situation. He almost had to bite his tongue to keep himself from speaking his thoughts.

Dear Reader,

I love quotes. It started back when I was a kid and my mother shared the "Prayer of Serenity" to help me keep life in perspective. Now, I have it taped to my computer and refer to it daily.

Another favorite is from Voltaire: "Perfect is the enemy of very good." It helps when I'm struggling to let go of something…say, a book I'm writing. I remember Voltaire's words and realize it will never be *perfect,* because nothing is *perfect.*

Jordana Fortune, this book's heroine, would've benefitted from Voltaire's advice. In her quest for perfection—being the perfect daughter, cultivating the perfect life, finding perfect love—she almost misses out on living. That is, until fate blows her into the arms of Tanner Redmond and turns her belief system upside down.

Along their journey, Tanner and Jordana realize the most perfect kind of love is imperfect; it encourages a person to be themself and knows that even on those very human bad days there's a safe haven in unconditional love.

Please drop me a line at nrobardsthompson@yahoo.com and let me know what you think of the story or share your favorite quotes.

Warmly,

Nancy

FORTUNE'S
UNEXPECTED
GROOM

NANCY ROBARDS
THOMPSON

Harlequin®

SPECIAL EDITION

If you purchased this book without a cover you should be aware that this book is stolen property. It was reported as "unsold and destroyed" to the publisher, and neither the author nor the publisher has received any payment for this "stripped book."

Special thanks and acknowledgment
to Nancy Robards Thompson for her contribution to
The Fortunes of Texas: Whirlwind Romance continuity.

ISBN-13: 978-0-373-65667-7

FORTUNE'S UNEXPECTED GROOM

Copyright © 2012 by Harlequin Books S.A.

Recycling programs
for this product may
not exist in your area.

All rights reserved. Except for use in any review, the reproduction or utilization of this work in whole or in part in any form by any electronic, mechanical or other means, now known or hereafter invented, including xerography, photocopying and recording, or in any information storage or retrieval system, is forbidden without the written permission of the publisher, Harlequin Enterprises Limited, 225 Duncan Mill Road, Don Mills, Ontario M3B 3K9, Canada.

This is a work of fiction. Names, characters, places and incidents are either the product of the author's imagination or are used fictitiously, and any resemblance to actual persons, living or dead, business establishments, events or locales is entirely coincidental.

This edition published by arrangement with Harlequin Books S.A.

For questions and comments about the quality of this book please contact us at Customer_eCare@Harlequin.ca.

® and TM are trademarks of Harlequin Books S.A., used under license. Trademarks indicated with ® are registered in the United States Patent and Trademark Office, the Canadian Trade Marks Office and in other countries.

www.Harlequin.com

Printed in U.S.A.

NANCY ROBARDS THOMPSON

Award-winning author Nancy Robards Thompson is a sister, wife and mother who has lived the majority of her life south of the Mason-Dixon line. As the oldest sibling, she reveled in her ability to make her brother laugh at inappropriate moments, and she soon learned she could get away with it by proclaiming "What? I wasn't doing anything." It's no wonder that upon graduating from college with a degree in journalism, she discovered that reporting "just the facts" bored her silly. Since hanging up her press pass to write novels full-time, critics have deemed her books "funny, smart and observant." She loves chocolate, champagne, cats and art (though not necessarily in that order). When she's not writing, she enjoys spending time with her family, reading, hiking and doing yoga.

This book is dedicated to talented ladies I worked with on this continuity: Karen Templeton, Marie Ferrarella, Judy Duarte, Susan Crosby and Allison Leigh.
Thanks for making this such a fun journey!
Also, Sarah McDaniel Dyer, for your great editing eye; and Gail Chasan and Susan Litman, because you're fabulous, fun and very wise.

Prologue

December 30, 2011

"What in the world possessed your family to try and fly out in the middle of a storm like this?" As Tanner Redmond closed the door, shutting out the storm, his eyes shone with a certain tenderness that made Jordana Fortune's pulse quicken. Despite having every reason to be angry with her—or at least at the situation she'd put them in—he didn't seem mad. In fact, as he crossed the room, wiping the rain off his face with both hands, he looked quite compassionate.

"I've asked myself the same question at least a dozen times."

He sat next to her on the worn couch—the only piece of furniture in the dilapidated hunting lodge, where the storm had forced them to seek shelter, the place where she'd dropped when her legs had given out after running for cover. Now, he was so close to her that their legs almost touched.

Almost.

But not quite.

Jordana's breath hitched and she fought her natural reflex to pull away, to reclaim her personal space. She'd met Tanner at her sister's wedding. The attraction had been instant. This evening, he'd stopped by the hotel to say goodbye.

She'd been so glad to see him.

The bad weather was the reason she'd initially refused to accompany her parents to the airport, opting instead to catch a later flight from Red Rock back to Atlanta once the weather improved. From the start, she'd had a bad feeling about the storm—no, more than a bad feeling. She'd been terrified. But she'd quickly changed her plans once Tanner had arrived at the hotel….

It had been a very long time since she'd met a man who'd made her want to change her mind once it was set. But he'd been on his way to the airport to batten down the hatches of his company, Redmond Flight School. She'd asked if he would drop her at the airport. All trepidation about flying during the tornado watch was shoved aside. Just so she could have a few more minutes with him.

Now, here they were. They could both be dead right now because of her impetuousness. If she hadn't detained him with the time it took to go back to her room to get her bags and check out, Tanner could've been safely at the airport instead of stuck in the middle of nowhere in this shack, his car in a ditch along the highway where he'd swerved to avoid a falling oak tree that had been uprooted by a gust of wind.

Why had she not honored her gut feeling and stayed put like she knew she should? What the heck was wrong with her?

She gazed up at Tanner—at the strong line of his square jaw, the masculine slope of his perfectly imperfect nose and the fullness of his mouth that might be a little feminine if not for the way it was counterbalanced by the imperfection of his nose. It looked like it might have been broken once. A keen awareness slowly started to burn in her innermost core.

Suddenly she knew exactly what her problem was. She was twenty-nine years old. Still a virgin.

She could've died tonight—still might if the storm spawned other tornadoes, which was a very real possibility. All the careful planning and saving herself for *the one* could very well amount to naught.

She'd saved herself and it was all coming down to this?

Suddenly, the cabin felt an awful lot like the bungalow Dorothy had ridden to Oz on the tail-winds of a similar storm. In fact, any minute she expected to see the wicked witch fly by on her broom, as the log hunting lodge lifted off for areas unknown.

And Jordana would die a virgin.

She shivered.

"Are you cold?" Tanner asked.

Before she could answer, he slid an arm around her shoulders and pulled her close. She melted into his warmth.

He smelled good and the hard flex of muscle against her softer curves felt even better. But the wind howled a mournful song. She could've sworn it was lamenting that they could both be dead by morning.

She shivered again and snuggled in closer, closing her eyes, wanting to disappear until the rain stopped and the wind quit howling.

A virgin... I am going to die a virgin.

"You're shaking," he said.

"Shh, don't talk. Just...hold me."

He closed the circle around her with his other arm, holding her tight. She nestled into his neck, breathing in the intoxicating smell of him—bergamot, leather and...something sexy and primal she couldn't label...something she was suddenly finding very hard to resist.

So, if she didn't want to die a virgin, why was she clinging to her virtue like a punctured life preserver?

Why... When Tanner Redmond was right here holding her so close?

Chapter One

April 20, 2012

Tanner Redmond had always believed the axiom *What doesn't kill you makes you stronger*. The fact that he was still alive after all he'd lived through proved he was one strong *sonuvabitch*. So why, then, was he afraid a baby might be his undoing?

He parked in a space in front of Jordana Fortune's condo in the Buckhead area of Atlanta. Sitting in the rental car for a moment, he tried to quiet the anger that had simmered inside him since he'd heard her voice on the phone less than twenty-four hours ago.

He drummed his fingers on the steering wheel. Had she really planned to keep this secret from him? What made her think she had the right?

He had no idea, but as soon as their conversation—which had gone nowhere—had ended, he had flown into Atlanta from Red Rock, Texas. Now that he was here in person, she wouldn't be able to put him off so easily. He intended to make it perfectly clear he wasn't going away.

With a quick jab of his thumb, he sprung the car's seat belt. He headed up the walk of pavers toward the hunter-green double doors set like a bruised eye in the middle of the stately, two-story red brick building.

He pulled back the brass door knocker and gave three sharp raps. It was slightly before seven o'clock in the morning. It was early, but his plan for the daybreak visit was to catch her before she went into work. She wasn't expecting him. He hadn't called before flying in because he wasn't about to give her warning, time to run, a chance to avoid him and the secret she'd already hidden for four months.

If not for Jordana's cousin, Victoria, who'd told him to call Jordana because she *desperately needed to talk to him,* he would still be blissfully unaware that the woman who'd blown him off after their one night was pregnant with his child.

The opening door drew him out of his inward brooding. There stood Jordana, looking shocked and so damned beautiful with her blond hair wet from her morning shower. Seeing her standing there in her bathrobe, with her face fresh and makeup-free, he didn't know whether he wanted to kiss her or put his fist through a wall.

"Tanner? What are you doing here?" She tugged at the sash of the robe, then crossed her arms over her ribs. The protective gesture pulled his gaze to her belly, which showed no signs of the child growing within. Of course, that big white terry robe wasn't exactly formfitting. It even swallowed up the prepregnancy curves that had been etched in his memory since that night... when they'd taken refuge from the storm. His eyes slowly made their way back to hers.

For one weak moment, seeing her again reminded him just how out of his league Jordana Fortune was. Not because her family had more money than European royalty, but her sheer presence—that mixture of grace and rock-solid strength—left him a little speechless.

Yeah, come to think of it, he'd been a little

speechless after she'd left him with a handshake and a no-nonsense "thanks for everything" the morning after they'd made love for the first and only time. That was the night the tornado had destroyed Red Rock and parts of San Antonio.

Nothing had been the same since. And given that he would be a father before the year was over, it was beginning to sink in that nothing would ever be the same again. It scared him to death because his own father hadn't been strong enough to be a family man. Tanner pushed the thought back into the dark recesses of his mind—the place where he stored his faded memories of the man who had once been his father and redoubled his vow that he would stand by his family no matter what.

"Seriously? You're asking me why I'm here?" His voice was a hoarse and throaty rasp. "You're pregnant with my child, Jordana. I wanted to see your face when you told me how long you thought you could keep that news from me."

Jordana sighed heavily and glanced around. He couldn't tell if her reaction was resignation or fear…fear of what? The neighbors finding out her little secret?

"Come in." She stepped back and motioned him through. He stepped onto the hardwood of the entryway and glanced around at the expensive-looking decor. High ceilings and vibrantly colored walls with paintings. The place was like a snapshot out of one of those architectural magazines. The day's first light was beginning to stream in through oversize windows that surrounded a large fireplace along the condo's back wall. Inviting and elegant. Just like Jordana. He would've expected nothing less of the crown princess of the Fortune South Enterprises dynasty.

"Look, I'm sorry, Tanner. You must've misunderstood our conversation yesterday. You didn't have to come." She closed the door, but kept her hand on the doorknob, as if she didn't expect him to stay very long. "You're under absolutely no obligation with this child. I don't need or want your help. I thought we had established that when we spoke."

Her cool words were a hot slap in his face. "I'm not here *for you*," he bit back. "I'm here for *my child*. And I intend to be involved in his life every step of the way."

She blanched. "*His* life?" Her right hand slid to her belly. "How do you know the baby is a boy?"

"I don't, but I intend to be there when we find out and for every other milestone in *our* kid's life. So, you might as well get used to that right now."

Tanner had been raised by a single mother who

sometimes worked two jobs to keep a roof over their heads and food on the table. She'd done a damn good job. His loser of a father had never paid a penny of child support. It was obvious Jordana didn't need his financial help in raising their child. But the thought that she'd considered cutting him out of his baby's life cut him to the core. His own father had been so absent from Tanner's and his siblings' lives that Tanner referred to him as "The Sperm Donor" rather than a father. As far as he was concerned, the name *father* or *dad* was a title earned by men who took their roles and responsibilities seriously. Tanner had always vowed he would be there for his kids…when the time came to have kids.

He just hadn't expected that time to be *right now*. Since leaving the Air Force seven years ago, he'd been married to his company, Redmond Flight School. Although he wanted kids *someday*—in the *very* distant future—a family of his own hadn't been on his radar. Well, that's what he got for having impulsive, unprotected sex with Jordana. He had been taking her to the airport so that she could meet her family and fly back to Atlanta with them. The Fortunes had chartered a flight to take them home after they'd all gathered in Red Rock for the wedding of Jordana's sister

Wendy Fortune to Marcos Mendoza. When Jordana had heard reports of a storm bearing down on Red Rock, she'd refused to fly out with her family. Then she'd changed her mind. Tanner had offered her a ride to the airport. They'd both been a little unnerved about being stranded out on the road when the tornado struck. And they'd both sought warmth and comfort in the other's arms. One thing led to another and… Well, you play, you pay.

"I know this is a hell of a time to ask, but were you not on birth control when we…?"

Stupid question. He realized it the minute the words passed his lips. The fact was further confirmed when sadness, or something just short of defeat, colored her golden-brown eyes. She shrugged and gestured toward the living room. "Sit down, Tanner. I need a cup of tea before I can deal with you at this hour. Do you prefer tea or coffee?"

He glared at her. *Deal with me?* "Coffee. But I don't want any."

She glared back. "How do you take yours?"

"I don't want to put you out."

"Well, I'm going to make it, anyway. So you'd be putting me out a lot less if you answered my question."

The woman was pigheaded as all get-out. "Okay. Fine. Black." At least he'd have her attention through the duration of a cup of joe, which he planned to nurse.

He watched her as she turned and padded barefoot, hips swaying under the cover of that big white robe, in the direction of what he presumed was the kitchen. He waited until she was out of his line of vision before he made his way into the living room and settled in a floral-print, over-stuffed armchair.

He raked his fingers through the close-cropped hair on his head. How could he have been so stupid? He didn't make a habit of having unprotected sex. Actually, he'd been so wrapped up in work lately, he hadn't had many opportunities for protected sex. Nonetheless, he didn't do it. For obvious reasons. But dammit, Jordana had been so aggressive that night. So wonderfully, deliciously insistent and responsive…only a dead man could've said no.

His body responded as he remembered that night. He sucked in a deep breath, fighting against arousal. Seeing her for the first time after all these months, with her clean morning face and her blond shoulder-length hair, slightly tussled as it started to dry, reminded him of why he hadn't been able to resist her. She was sexy as hell, of course he hadn't refused her. God almighty, despite the mess they were in, he even wanted her now.

He leaned forward in the chair, bracing his forearms on his knees, lacing his fingers loosely together. Maybe there really was a thin line between love and hate. Well, *desire* and hate, he quickly corrected. He didn't know her well enough to be in love with her...no matter what his body was trying to tell him. Obviously, he didn't really hate her, either. He was upset and more than a little angry at how things had turned out.

That had him focusing on the darker side of the *desire*-and-hate equation. The clear-cut side. His emotions might be muddled right now, but the one thing he knew for a fact was he hated the way Jordana had hidden his child from him. Anger coursed through his veins and clarified his momentary confusion.

He would stick to his plan. He would not leave Atlanta until she agreed to marry him and come back to Red Rock, Texas. His child would not be born illegitimate. Come hell or Jordana Fortune, he would do the right thing.

Jordana drew enough water in the kettle for a cup of tea for herself and a cup of coffee for

Tanner. Her hand shook as she measured the French roast into the press-pot coffeemaker. The smell of the grounds—mixed with the thought of Tanner Redmond sitting in her living room with a stubborn set to his square jaw and a wild look in his chocolate-brown eyes made her stomach pitch. She held her breath for a moment, hoping to tamp down the awful sensation.

Smells she'd loved prepregnancy—like coffee and her favorite perfume—nearly turned her inside out now. Even so, enduring the stench of coffee was a small price to pay for an excuse to get away from Tanner for a few moments to gather her thoughts. Because the man who had been so gentle and patient with her back in December seemed like an entirely different animal now. She had about four minutes to figure out how she was going to change his mind and send him on his way.

Jordana stiffened as the wave of nausea swelled and tried to crest, despite the fact that there was nothing left in her stomach. She drew in a deep breath—in through her nose, out through her mouth. She repeated the process until her stomach finally settled. Morning sickness had plagued her since the second month of the pregnancy. In fact, it was her first clue that something different was going on with her body. Her doctor assured her the symptoms would go away in the second trimester, but so far, no luck. She'd been *blessed* with the variety of morning ills that sometimes lingered well into the afternoon. Today felt like it would be one of those days. It had been hard enough to drag herself into work and hide the fact that she was under the weather. People started to take notice when, for lack of a better excuse, she blamed her condition on rotating bouts of the flu and extreme exhaustion. Both excuses had worn thin a while ago. Now, what she didn't need was for Tanner to come waltzing in and blow her cover.

She could just kill her cousin Victoria for spilling the beans to Tanner even after Jordana had explicitly told her she wasn't ready to face him. In her trademark fashion, Victoria had pushed the issue, badgering Jordana, claiming she should just bite the bullet and tell him now because there would never be a perfect time to break news like this. Jordana should've known in Victoria-speak, her cousin was actually saying, "If you don't tell him, I will." The woman had never been able to keep a secret. When Victoria got something in her head, inevitably, it ended up rolling right off her tongue.

Jordana glanced at the clock. It was about six-fifteen in Texas. She had a sudden urge to pick up the phone and give the busybody a piece of her mind. But the kettle whistled, alerting her that the water was ready. She poured the water over the ground coffee in the press pot and over the tea bag in her favorite mug, setting the timer so both could steep for three minutes.

She'd talk to Victoria later, and when she did, her cousin was going to get a piece of Jordana's mind, the likes of which she'd never seen before.

Jordana already knew what her cousin would say.... "Perhaps I was wrong to move things along the way I did, but really, Jordana, I've done you a huge favor."

The last time they had spoken, Victoria had been spouting nonsense about how she believed that Jordana's marriage to Tanner was inevitable. That they belonged together in the same way Victoria and her fiancé, Garrett, did. Victoria swore she could feel it in her bones. What her cousin didn't realize was just because she and Garrett fell in love didn't mean it would work out for Jordana and Tanner.

Tanner simply didn't see her "that way." If he did, he would've called her during the past four months. But he hadn't. Not even once.

As she watched the timer tick down the remaining minute before she had to go back into the living room and face Tanner, she knew she needed to come up with a plan.

Think...

After one night together, she didn't know him very well. They'd danced and made small talk the evening of Wendy and Marcos's wedding. It was enough time to form the conclusion that he probably was a decent guy. A decent guy who'd followed up on his responsibility after her cousin spilled the beans.

She needed to let him know he was released from all obligation. Off the hook. Dismissed. She had a sinking feeling nice guys didn't walk away from their duty that easily.

The timer dinged. She plunged the press pot's filter, then poured the steaming brew into a large ceramic mug and carried it and her tea around the corner into the living room with what she hoped was confident ease.

It was time to face the music. The sooner they got down to business, the sooner Tanner Redmond headed back to Texas and out of her life.

He sat up straighter in the chair as she approached, but not before she'd glimpsed the slump of his shoulders that belied the burden he was carrying. He looked big and bulky and slightly out of place folded into the floral-print chair. And really handsome, she thought, before she caught herself.

"Here you go." She handed him the mug. "I don't mean to be rude, but I'm due in the office for a conference call in less than an hour and I still have to get dressed. So drink up."

He lifted his eyebrows but held her gaze. "I didn't come here to drink coffee. Though I do appreciate you making it for me—"

"I know. So, let's cut to the chase. You're here because my cousin Victoria made you believe I need your help. I don't. I may be pregnant, but I'm not *in trouble*. I'm going to have this baby, and you are under absolutely no obligation to me or to the child." She paused and drew in a deep breath, hoping to quell another wave of nausea. "I think that covers just about everything."

She remained standing, hoping he'd take the hint. Instead, he took a long sip from the mug. "Mmm…good coffee."

Seriously? Irritation skittered along her nerves. "Tanner, did you hear what I said?"

He nodded. "Yeah, I heard you. But what you don't seem to understand is this isn't just *your* child. It's mine, too. You may think you have it all under control, but you need to know right now.

I'm not leaving here until you agree to marry me. Because no child of mine will be born out of wedlock."

"Marry you?" she squeaked.

He watched the emotions play out on her face. First, confusion. Next, a look that resembled something just short of horror. Then the color faded from her cheeks, leaving her deathly pale. Despite the spectrum of emotion, the stubborn set of her jaw never eased.

So, she was going to make this hard on both of them. Didn't she understand it could be so simple? Really. All she had to do was the *right thing* and agree to marry him, and then he'd leave—for the moment, anyway. She could get dressed, go to the office for her phone meeting—or whatever it was she needed to do—while he made arrangements with a notary or the justice of the peace to marry them right here in Atlanta. They would make their union legal sooner rather than later. For the sake of the baby.

Or maybe because he wanted to pin her down now before she managed to slip away again like she did the last time he saw her. The morning after the storm, he'd taken her to find her family and she'd left him with a handshake. A handshake and a "Thanks…for everything." He'd known his share of women—spent the night with more than a few—but none had ever shaken his hand the morning after.

"Look, Tanner, you can't just waltz into my home and expect me to marry you." She looked exasperated. "Do you really think that's the answer to this…this…situation?"

So, that's what she wanted to call it. He looked at her for a moment, weighing his words. "Who else knows about our little *situation?*"

She crossed her arms over her ribs, pressing the robe against her frame. She didn't look pregnant, but then again, he had no idea how far along women were when they started showing.

"No one else knows I'm pregnant, and I'd like to keep it that way. For now, at least."

"Well, they're going to find out eventually. Don't you think it would be better to hear it from you…or us? Do you have any idea what it was like to learn that the woman I hadn't spoken to in four months was pregnant with my child? Jordana, why didn't you tell me before Victoria forced your hand? Why didn't you call?"

She shifted her weight from one foot to the other, looking a little guilty. "I've only known I was pregnant for about three months."

She was hedging. "Three months is long enough. Why didn't you tell me?"

"I guess I was afraid. So many pregnancies don't make it past the first trimester. I just didn't want to alarm you."

"Alarm me?" he said. "Were you ever going to fill me in?"

Her mouth held that stubborn line, but then he realized her brown eyes were swimming with tears. "I'm sorry," she said. "I never meant for this to happen."

The hard-nosed approach to getting Tanner Redmond out of her condo hadn't worked. But the tears did. Jordana wasn't an actress. The waterworks were genuine, compliments of the perfect storm of pregnancy hormones and frustration that consumed her all at once. It hit like an emotional tidal wave crashing down on her before she could run for cover.

After that, Tanner had easily agreed to give her time to think, time to get dressed so she could make her meeting on time—but only after she'd agreed to meet him for lunch tomorrow—Saturday, her day off.

She lifted the mug of naturally decaffeinated English breakfast tea and sipped at it tentatively, unsure of how her stomach would respond. But it was her conscience that felt ill. She'd decided the best way to let him off the hook was if she unexpectedly got "called out of town" tomorrow.

Jordana had decided she'd be doing Tanner a favor by doing this. Her administrative assistant, Marta, would call and deliver the news later this afternoon. She'd tell him, *No, unfortunately, she was not certain when Jordana would return.*

That meant there would be no way Tanner, who had a business to run back in Red Rock, would be able to wait for her in Atlanta. He'd have to get back to tend to his flight school. Once he was able to put some distance between them and think things out rationally, he'd realize getting married was not the answer. They'd work out a visitation schedule—one of the perks of Tanner being a pilot was he'd be able to fly in and see his child as often as he liked. By that time, he'd see that marriage was just an unnecessary burden to place on everyone involved.

She straightened a stack of papers on her desk, beginning her daily tidying-up ritual early. Because she planned on leaving early. She was indeed going to take herself out of town. She'd take her laptop and the files her father had asked her to read through and go to her favorite bed-and-breakfast on St. Simons Island. The time away at the beach would do her a world of good. Not to mention, she wouldn't have to ask Marta to lie to Tanner. Truly, she would be out of town—on business.

He could rest assured that he made a valiant effort, but he would know full well that he was absolved of any and all obligation to her and the baby.

Jordana stared out her office window on the twenty-second floor, high above Peachtree Street. The breathtaking view of downtown Atlanta did little to soothe her. The shiny, mirrored buildings only seemed to reflect the fact that running away to the beach didn't make the real challenge go away. Eventually, she would have to break the news to her parents. The mere thought turned her stomach inside out. She put a protective hand on her belly. Maybe what she was feeling was the remnants of the morning sickness. She glanced at her desk clock. It was nearly noon. She needed some nourishment, needed to feed the baby something other than saltine crackers. She wrote a reminder to herself on a Post-it note to follow up on an idea she wanted to present to her father before she left for St. Simons—the idea stemmed from a lead he had mentioned. Maybe if she proved just how conscientious she was at work, he would be more accepting of the news that she was about to become a single parent.

The buzz of the phone intercom startled her and made her drop her pen.

"Ms. Fortune," said Marta. "There's a gentleman here to see you."

Jordana's heart hiccupped. She wasn't expecting anyone, but she had a dread-filled hunch she knew just who it might be.

"Thank you, Marta. Does this gentleman have a name?" She purposely softened her voice so not to *shoot the messenger*.

Marta was quiet for a few beats before she said, "Yes, ma'am. He says his name is Tanner Redmond."

Chapter Two

For a very brief moment, Jordana contemplated an escape plan. It was a crazy idea, of course. Tanner was standing right in front of Marta and had heard her talking to Jordana. Escaping or pretending she wasn't in the office was not an option. But it didn't mean she had to make herself available to him.

She just needed a moment to think....

"Marta, would you please ask Mr. Redmond to have a seat in the lobby? I'm in the middle of something and I need to get to a stopping point. Please tell him I'll be out to see him in a few minutes."

"Certainly, Miss Fortune."

Jordana sat in silence, rubbing her right temple. The last thing she needed was to argue with Tanner about their *situation,* right here in the office. The more she thought about the way he'd just barged in here, the more it irritated her. Really, it was pretty darn presumptuous of him to just show up. But maybe that was his way. After all, hadn't he appeared unannounced on her doorstep at daybreak, expecting her to receive him in a moment's notice?

Then again, she had set the tone for those *instant expectations*. One-night stands tended to give a guy the green light to bypass the basics of common courting courtesies and slide directly into home plate.

A pang of guilt squeezed her heart. It just figured, didn't it? The first time she had sex—the one time—she'd gotten pregnant. The thought made her feel sick, but this time it had nothing to do with morning sickness. The reason she couldn't bear to face him went much deeper than one-night-stand regret. Yes, every time she looked at him she remembered how out of her mind she'd been that night of the hurricane...out of her mind because she was afraid she was going to die in the midst of a tornado, never having made love to a man.

Until that night with Tanner, Jordana had been a virgin.

And Tanner didn't even know that she had given him the most precious gift she had to give a man. A part of herself she'd guarded jealously, because it was reserved for the man who would be the love of her life. That's why she'd been a twenty-nine-year-old virgin when she'd met Tanner.

She closed her eyes against the memory, as if squeezing them tight enough might obliterate the mental images of the way she'd thrown herself at him. She hadn't even been aware that she had the power to seduce a man.

She placed her hand on her stomach. Giving him that part of herself had led to another gift... a baby that would tie them together. Forever. Whether they got married or not.

She pressed her fingertips over her closed eyelids and tried to obliterate the image of herself in Tanner's arms. When that didn't work, she opened her eyes and forced her mind onto a different train of thought.

Maybe Tanner had come to the office to tell her he'd changed his mind. Jordana sat up straighter in her chair. *Yes, that was better.* Maybe he had to go back to Red Rock earlier than expected, and had come to say goodbye…?

As much as she wanted to believe it, she knew inherently it wasn't so. He'd been too persistent that morning. So persistent, in fact, he'd almost been convincing…that they could get married and be a family…the three of them. That somehow love could bloom in the shadow of a marriage in name only.

A life built on a foundation of resentment held together by a mortar of obligation and duty.

She drummed her manicured fingers on the desk. Why was Tanner so eager, when he hadn't even cared enough to call her since they'd said goodbye in late December? Was she selling her child short by not even considering the possibility of a life with Tanner?

The thought turned the skin on her arms to gooseflesh.

Could it work? She'd been so embarrassed seeing Tanner again for the first time since *that night,* she hadn't even allowed herself to think about possibility and hope. That she and Tanner might be able to get married first and learn to love each other later.

Her pulse beat in her ears like a ticking bomb,

and for a moment, she let herself go there. She imagined living together as a family, spending holidays together, rather than alternating time with their child as dictated by a custody agreement, celebrating all those milestones in their child's life that Tanner had insisted he would be there for, whether she liked it or not. She imagined waking up in his bed—their bed—every morning. And then the reality bomb exploded when Tanner was absent from her vision. Instead, she saw herself waking up alone; he was nowhere to be found because he didn't love her...or maybe it was because she didn't love him.

Tanner wanted to marry her. Yet, he didn't even know her. Not in the the-man-I-marry-will-know-all-about-me-and-still-love-me-despite-myself sort of way.

The way she'd always dreamed her marriage would be.

Jordana wanted to do right by her child and give the baby the best possible life. But agreeing to a loveless marriage simply wouldn't be what was best for the child. The realization brought with it the kind of sadness that made her heart ache down to its very center.

She'd been so careful her entire life, saving herself for just the right man, and one careless move

had changed *everything*. All her life she'd dreamed
of falling in love and having a family of her own.
In those dreams the man she loved had loved her
back with a ferocity that could move mountains.
If she agreed to Tanner's impulsive, loveless plan,
they would end up hating each other, and the one
who would suffer the most would be their child.

Suddenly, what she needed to do was perfectly
clear. She needed to have a frank conversation
with Tanner—right now, outside of the office—
and set things straight once and for all. The sooner
he was on a plane back to Red Rock, the better off
everyone would be.

John Michael Fortune had a bad reputation of
being a hard-ass. But Tanner knew from personal
experience a person didn't get to Mr. Fortune's
station in life without being strong willed and
having a clear-focused vision of what he wanted.

That's why when John Michael entered the
lobby as Tanner waited for Jordana, he greeted
her father like an old family friend. Tanner had
spoken with the Atlanta Fortune patriarch only
on a handful of occasions, and was much closer to
the Fortunes of his own generation, such as Scott
Fortune, Jordana's brother. But to his pleasant surprise, John Michael rewarded Tanner's fortitude

with a hardy clap on the back and a firm handshake.

"Tanner Redmond, good to see you," he said.

"Mr. Fortune," Tanner returned.

He hoped John Michael's greeting was the beginning of a long and amiable relationship. Because it would make life much easier for everyone involved if he and the grandfather of his child were on solid terms.

"How's business?" John Michael asked. "I heard Redmond Flight School took a beating in that tornado."

"Business has never been better." Tanner stood a little taller reporting this news, because it was true. "It was rough in the days following the storm, especially after one of my flight instructors, Gary Tompkins, died. But we worked hard and pulled everything together. Business had to carry on. I'm sure you know how that is."

John Michael nodded. "I was sorry to hear Gary died. Scott told me he was a real asset to Redmond Flight School. But you have a good attitude. So is everything rebuilt and repaired?"

"Sure is. In fact, I'm looking into expanding. I want to begin offering charter services before the end of the year. I have a line on a Cessna Citation that's on the market for a reasonable price. If I get it, I'm going to hire a crew and a pilot."

John Michael's right brow arched. "Sounds ambitious, but it also sounds like you know your stuff. I'm sure you have everything under control. What brings you to Atlanta? Are you here on business?"

Mustering his most sincere smile, Tanner responded, "I'm here to see Jordana. I'm taking her to lunch."

John Michael did a double take and furrowed his brow.

"I didn't realize you and my daughter were seeing each other." The look on the older man's face did not suggest objection; surprise and puzzlement, maybe, but not dissent. "Red Rock to Atlanta is quite a commute for a lunch date. Is this relationship serious? That daughter of mine never tells her mother and me anything."

Tanner worried the button at the cuff of his blue oxford shirt as he considered how to answer the question. That's when it hit him: his best chance at getting Jordana to marry him was standing right in front of him. If her father was on board with the wedding, Jordana would be more likely to agree. He looked the man square in his brown eyes—a feature Jordana had inherited from her father.

"Yes, sir, I believe we are serious. In fact, one of the reasons I've come all this way is to ask you a very important question—actually, I'd like to talk to you before I take Jordana to lunch. Would you happen to have a moment now, or should I make an appointment with you?"

John Michael's expression suddenly sobered and he studied Tanner as if searching for weakness. Tanner redoubled his resolve to carry through with what he knew he had to do.

"Please hold my calls," John Michael instructed the receptionist. "Come to my office, Tanner."

Tanner let out a breath he hadn't realized he'd been holding. He reminded himself that despite the man's formidable reputation, he'd seemed easy enough to get along with. Of course, that was before John Michael realized Tanner had his eye on Jordana. Tanner could only hope his future father-in-law would be this even-tempered once he learned exactly how *serious* his and Jordana's relationship had become.

Jordana made her way out to the lobby to collect Tanner, but when she got there he was gone. She glanced around the empty reception area.

"Where did he go?" she asked Marta. "Did he leave?"

"No, he's in your father's office."

"What?" Jordana's heart constricted then lodged in her windpipe. She had to clear her throat before she could muster a calm voice and ask, "How long have they been in there?"

Marta squinted at the clock on the wall, then pushed a strand of brown hair off her forehead. "Not very long. Your father arrived shortly after I buzzed you to let you know Mr. Redmond had arrived. Mr. Fortune asked me to hold all calls, but I'm sure he wouldn't mind if I buzzed him to say you're looking for him and Mr. Redmond."

Jordana stared out the floor-to-ceiling windows along the office's front wall as the ramifications of what might be happening—that Tanner might be telling her father about the baby before she could—settled around her. The gorgeous view of the Atlanta skyline seemed to tilt a little. She steadied herself on the edge of the reception desk and shifted her gaze to the leather chairs in the waiting area.

"No, that's okay. I'll just wait until they're finished."

Like heck she'd wait. What in the world was Tanner doing in her father's office? Well, there was only one way to find out.

As soon as she was out of Marta's line of sight,

Jordana speed-walked down the parquet-covered hallway toward her father's office, her high heels tap-tapping on the wood. In the process, she nearly ran into the intern, who was looking down at a stack of papers as he stepped out of the copy room.

"Oh, excuse me," he said. "I'm sorry, Miss Fortune. I wasn't watching where I was going."

She mustered her best smile and kept walking as she said, "No problem, Ben. I was... I'm sorry, too."

When she reached her father's office door, she paused before she knocked, composing in her head what she'd say to them.

Well, it would depend on her father's demeanor. If he was in a good mood, then Tanner hadn't betrayed her; if he was in a bad mood...it was a good thing she could run in heels. But then there would be the moral dilemma whether she should check on Tanner, because if he spilled the beans, her father would surely kill him.

And if her dad didn't, she would.

Before she could knock, the door opened and she was standing in front of her father. Tanner, she noted, was a few paces behind him—still standing. No visible bodily harm.

For a moment that seemed to last a lifetime,

Jordana held her breath as she gauged her father's mood.

"Jordana, there you are." He smiled.

Jordana exhaled. *Good mood.* He was in a good mood. *Oh, thank God.*

"Hi, Dad," she said, infusing her smile with all the enthusiasm she could muster. "What are you doing?"

"I was just having a nice talk with Tanner."

As if on cue, Tanner stepped out from behind John Michael, pulled Jordana into his arms and planted a kiss on her lips. For a split second, her body responded to him—to the sheer depth and breadth of the way his big body encircled her, just possessive enough to make her knees go a little weak. Her lips parted in response. The taste of him, the feel of his lips on hers reminded her of how good he'd tasted *that night*. How much she'd wanted him—

She managed to wedge both hands between them, ready to shove him away, but before she could, he pulled back and smiled down at her. If she didn't know better, she might have thought that the way he looked at her…meant something.

"Hello, darling," he said. "I've missed you."

Darling?

"What the heck, Tanner?" She dragged the back

of her hand across her mouth, trying to erase the feel of his lips on hers.

John Michael frowned at her. "Jordana. That's not a very nice greeting. Tanner flew in all the way from Red Rock to take you to lunch. What's wrong with you this morning?"

What was wrong? Oh, if he only knew. Well, at least his asking that question suggested he *didn't* know, and that was enough to help Jordana regain her bearings. But then again, her father had a great poker face. He wasn't about to cause a scene in the office. But one thing was perfectly clear: her father seemed to think that she and Tanner were… together. A couple. She had no idea what nonsense Tanner had been flinging at her dad, but common sense dictated that she play along—at least for now—so that her father didn't get suspicious. At least until she could *break up with him* over lunch.

"What are you doing here, *darling?*" she said to Tanner. "You're a day early. I was expecting to see you *tomorrow.*" Jordana gritted her molars as she smiled.

Tanner grinned back, obviously game to play along. "Oh, I know, *sweetheart.*" His Texas drawl seemed exaggerated—or at least she'd never no-ticed it before now. "I missed you so much, I couldn't wait another day. I decided to surprise you."

"Well, yes, you certainly surprised me. What were you and Daddy talking about behind closed doors?"

She looked back and forth between Tanner and her father, who looked eerily smug…like he knew a secret. So she shifted her gaze to Tanner.

He smiled at her, and against her will, something in his eyes pulled her in. The same way it had when they'd danced at the wedding. Just as it had that day of the storm when she'd initially decided not to fly home with her family—because her gut instinct warned her of imminent danger. Then Tanner had stopped by the house that morning to say goodbye to everyone. After her family had left, she'd changed her mind and decided to join them after she'd learned he was on his way to the airport. Wanting to spend just a little more time with him, she'd gone against her instincts and better judgment. She'd been reeled in by the same…what was it…a look? His presence?

She'd been so shocked to see him this morning—and a bit humiliated to face him—that she'd been immune to his charms. But now, it was all coming back.

"We had a nice talk." Tanner nodded. "Man-to-man. Spent some time getting to know each other."

Her father was being eerily quiet. Something she couldn't remember seeing ever in her entire life. He was letting Tanner take the upper hand, which was just downright weird.

"Yes, we did," her father said. "I'm so grateful that Tanner was there to take care of you the night of the storm, Jordana." He turned back to Tanner. "My other daughter Wendy might be a little scattered, but sometimes Jordana is a little too introspective for her own good. If she'd listened to us and just come with us to the airport like we'd planned, she wouldn't have found herself in a mess and dragged you into it, too. But I guess it all worked out in the end."

A mess? Jordana was paralyzed for a heartbeat. Did her father know about the baby? Of course he didn't. The only way he could know was if Victoria told him. She may have blabbed to Tanner, but she wouldn't dare tell her father. Would she?

Jordana took a deep breath and reframed the situation. If her father knew that Tanner Redmond had gotten her pregnant, he would not be standing here being so uncharacteristically personable. Cautiously, she gazed up at her father. He was a good head taller than she was—and so was

Tanner, for that matter. Facing off, the two men seemed at once imposing yet somehow equally matched. At least right now. It would be a different story once her father found out. If Tanner knew what was good for him, he'd get as far away from here as possible before that happened. She was keeping this baby. She was raising her or him on her own. She wouldn't sell out to a loveless sham of a marriage.

That was her final answer.

In an uncharacteristic burst of defiance, Jordana blurted, "If you'd listened to me in the first place, Daddy, none of us would've been in danger. I told you I didn't think we should fly that day, that we should wait. But no. No one would listen to me."

The words were spewing like the morning sickness that had seized her body the past few months. She couldn't stop it; she knew if she tried she'd choke on the resentment. "If you listened to me every once in a while maybe a lot of things would be different."

Whoa! She clamped her mouth shut before she said any more. Neither Victoria nor Tanner had told on her, but if she didn't exercise a little self-control, she was going to tell on herself. Suddenly regretting her outburst, she braced for the inevitable backlash from her father. No one but no one talked back to John Michael Fortune without suffering the consequences.

Oddly, he stood squinting down at her with a neutral, if slightly bemused, look on his face. He shook his head and turned to Tanner. "Take her out to a nice, long lunch. In fact, Jordana, take the rest of the afternoon off. You obviously need a break."

"I don't want—"

"Jordana." Her father silenced her with a single booming word. All traces of his earlier bemusement gone, replaced by the stern glare that was famous for making grown men cry. "Leave. Now. I don't want to see you back in this office until Monday morning."

John Michael shook Tanner's hand. "It was a pleasure, but I need to get back to work. I'm sure we will be talking again soon." He glanced at Jordana, but directed his words at Tanner. "Good luck, son. She's been in a very strange mood lately."

Jordana snorted, but before she could say anything, her father did something so uncharacteristic it nearly rendered Jordana speechless, anyway. He hugged her and planted a fatherly kiss on her cheek. Something else Jordana couldn't recall him doing in recent memory.

Her heart sank low in her chest. What in the world had Tanner told him?

Chapter Three

Tanner and Jordana didn't speak as they walked out of the office and into the mahogany-paneled elevator bank. She didn't have to say a word for him to recognize she was furious. He could feel her anger radiating off her in waves as they waited for an elevator to arrive to carry them down twenty-two stories to the ground floor.

Tanner decided if he didn't break the tension, Jordana might burst.

"Your father is a great guy."

Jordana shot him a look.

"Really? Nice?" Jordana asked. "I've heard him

described a lot of ways, but *nice* isn't an adjective people usually use when they talk about John Michael Fortune."

"I enjoyed talking to him."

Jordana turned and faced him, eyes narrowed. "Yeah, about that—" The elevator interrupted her by announcing its arrival with a loud *ding*.

They entered the empty car, and as it started its descent, Jordana tore into him.

"What the heck are you doing, Tanner? Why did you come here and what did you tell my father?"

Her cheeks were flushed and her eyes glistened with fury. He couldn't remember seeing her look more beautiful. Healthy and vital…and pregnant with his child.

"You know why I came. Do you really want to talk about it here?" he asked.

"Well, yes, because I don't know where else we would talk about it. When we get off this elevator, I'm getting in my car and going home. You are getting back on your plane—or however you got here—and going back to Red Rock."

"Actually, I was thinking we could go grab some lunch."

Her lips puckered with annoyance. "Are you listening to me?"

The elevator stopped on the first floor and the doors slid open, revealing the marble-and-brass lobby. A fountain in the center cascaded soft ambient noise. They stepped out of the car and Jordana stopped right outside the elevator doors. "I'm going home, Tanner. Alone. If you'd like to tell me what you and my father talked about, this is your chance. If not, frankly, I guess it doesn't matter. I don't have the energy to play guessing games with you."

Tanner glanced around the professional building's lobby. A handful of people walked with a purpose toward the exit. Others, talking on cell phones and carrying briefcases, entered the building, branching off in various directions. About three yards to the left of where they stood, two men lingered by the elevator banks, deep in conversation.

"You really want to do this here?" he asked.

"It's up to you," she said, an edge to her voice. "Speak now or forever hold your peace."

"Funny you should say that." He chuckled, hoping some levity would lighten her mood. "Because I just asked your father for your hand in marriage. I told him I was here in Atlanta to propose to you. He told me he thought it was the best idea he'd heard in ages."

* * *

For the first time in her life, Jordana knew what it was like to see stars after being verbally sucker punched. It was the strangest sensation, and once she got her bearings, she wanted to kick Tanner Redmond. She wanted to scream at him until he admitted that everything he'd just told her was a cruel joke, that he'd never play so dirty he would force her into marriage by going over her head to her father.

But when she opened her mouth to tell him this, all that came out was a giant sob. Because despite the fact that she was twenty-nine years old, financially secure and fiercely independent, her father's word was still law. It was that way for all her brothers and sisters, too. No matter how old the Fortune siblings got, John Michael Fortune still ruled the clan with an iron fist.

"Aww, no, Jordana. No, please don't cry," Tanner pleaded.

His words made everything worse.

"How dare you—" She choked on another sob and turned toward the exit, walking as fast as she could to get away from him. *Breathe,* she reminded herself. She drew in a few gulps of air, trying to stop the deluge of tears.

Just because her father *thought it was the best*

idea he'd heard in ages didn't mean the marriage was inevitable.

Yeah, keep telling yourself that.

"Please, wait," Tanner called, trailing after her.

When he caught up to her, she hissed, "How could you? Going to my father behind my back was just…dirty pool."

He matched her step for step. "Look, I'm sorry. I didn't tell him *everything*. You know…" He gestured toward her belly.

"You didn't? Why not? Were you afraid that he might tell you exactly what I've been saying all along—that a loveless marriage is doomed from the start? That it's the worst possible thing to do to a child? You know he would never support such a farce." Jordana stopped suddenly in front of the exit. "So, what did you say to him? Did you lie and tell him you were in love with me?"

The words spilled out of Jordana's mouth before she could stop them. Along with them was the most peculiar sense of…hope. For a split second she wanted him to say…*yes*. She wanted to hear him profess his love because maybe then, just maybe, there would be a chance for them. The moment seemed to be isolated in a bubble where she saw her life flash before her eyes: he loved her, she loved him, they were a happy couple…a family. And for a millisecond she wanted nothing more.

But then Tanner shrugged and the bubble burst, revealing what Jordana thought was a hint of panic in his dark eyes.

"Not exactly." A note of defensiveness colored his voice.

She felt her cheeks flame with resentment and humiliation. Her guard slammed back into place like a steel door.

What had she expected him to say? That he'd fallen madly, deeply in love with her over the months they hadn't even spoken? Of course not, hence the *loveless marriage* part to which she objected so vehemently. The very odd thing she found almost as unsettling as his rejection was the fact that during that *perfect bubble* moment, she'd hoped he would say he loved her.

How ridiculous was that?

They were back to square one.

"Goodbye, Tanner."

She stepped into the vestibule of the rotating glass door, and Tanner grabbed her hand as he entered the carousel, and despite how she tried to shake him off, he stuck close behind her. That's when Jordana noticed two women who worked on the same floor as her entering the building on the other side of the revolving door. She tried to keep her head down, but not before she saw them look at her, then at each other, concerned, as if they were trying to decide whether or not she needed help.

Great. Just what she needed. She didn't know them by name; but since they had offices on the same floor, they were all three on friendly greeting terms.

She'd better get out of here fast before she made an even bigger spectacle of herself. Still, even if they did call security, she didn't plan to stick around in the parking lot long enough for the guard to come to her rescue…as if he could help her. No one could save her from this situation. No, she would walk this path alone.

Tears streamed down Jordana's face as she beelined for her car. It was the sort of ugly cry that racked her whole body with sobs. She didn't know how to make it stop. It was as if she were possessed by an alien that had taken control of her emotions.

Tanner walked beside her, strangely quiet. The only sound was the distant whirr of traffic on Peachtree Street, on the opposite side of the building from where they were. As they made their way toward her car, Tanner offered her a crisp white handkerchief, which she ignored.

Instead, she went for her purse to pull out a tissue and her car keys. That's when she realized her purse was in her office.

Jordana made another herky-jerky stop in the middle of the parking lot. The woman was more unpredictable than a bucking bronco.

"What's wrong?" he asked tentatively, bracing himself for another verbal lashing, which he probably deserved. She was right, going to her father had been dirty pool. But when it came down to his child and whether or not he would be allowed to be a part of the baby's life, no moves were off-limits.

"My car keys are upstairs in the office."

Jordana bit her bottom lip. Her nose was red and her makeup had created dark, streaky smudges on her cheeks, but the tears glistening in her eyes highlighted gorgeous gold and amber flecks. She looked vulnerable in a way that made him want to gather her in his arms and protect her from the world.

But he didn't dare touch her, for fear that she would lash out again. All this emotion couldn't be good for the baby. He needed to help her calm down.

Again, he offered her the handkerchief, a white flag, a peace offering...of sorts. To his great relief, this time she accepted it. She swiped the linen cloth over her face, then wiped her nose.

"I must look a mess," she said.

"You're beautiful," he answered, and he meant it.

She shook her head, and he thought he glimpsed the tortured dullness of defeat in her dark eyes.

"Come on," he said. "I'm parked over here. Let's get out of here."

She didn't protest. In fact, she took the arm he offered and allowed him to lead her to the rental car, which was parked a few feet away.

He helped her into the front seat on the passenger's side of the car and then walked around and situated himself behind the wheel.

"What kind of food are you in the mood for?" he asked.

"None. I'm not hungry. My stomach is upset."

"It's been an emotional morning. I'm sorry about that."

She looked at him for the first time since they'd gotten into the car. "You're sorry about what? That you went over my head to my father to get your way?"

He weighed his words, determined to tell the

truth, but not wanting to say anything to make the situation worse. "I'm really sorry that my meeting with your father upset you. That wasn't my intention. I just felt like you'd already made up your mind, that you weren't going to give me a choice about whether I would be a part of my child's life. I didn't know how else to make you see how important that is to me."

He heard her quick intake of breath.

"Jordana, this is my child...*our child.* I want to be there for the baby and for you. Will you please give me a chance? Can we please go have some lunch and talk about it?"

She wasn't looking at him now. She was staring out the window, her right arm propped on the window ledge, her chin resting on her fist. But he sensed that she was calmer. At least she wasn't threatening to leave the car.

"Go ahead," she said, "talk. Frankly, I don't have the energy to fight with you right now."

"How long is the morning sickness supposed to last?"

She straightened in the seat, facing forward now. "It was supposed to end with the first trimester, but it looks like I've gotten an extra helping."

He tensed. "Is that normal? I mean, have you

talked to the doctor about it? To make sure the baby is okay?"

"Yes, I've been getting good prenatal care. The doctor says everything is fine. I've lived with morning sickness for the past three months. So it's sort of becoming a way of life, but it zaps me. In fact, that was my first clue that something was... different."

"Maybe it's what you're eating. Or what you're not eating. What have you had to eat today?"

She pulled down the car's sun visor and cringed at herself in the mirror. "Tea and saltine crackers," she said, as she used her fingers to fix her makeup. "It's the only thing I can keep down."

"No wonder you're so weak. You need to get something in your stomach. That might make you feel better."

He started the car, half waiting for her to protest, but, again to his surprise, she didn't.

"Well, yeah, there's that compounded by the nerves of having just told off my father. I hate this. I am a mess of hormones and I really don't know what to do."

"Your dad will be fine," he said.

She frowned at him. "Obviously, you don't know him very well. No one talks to him that way and gets away with it. He might seem fine right now, but there will be hell to pay later."

"Not if you stick with me," Tanner insisted.

Out of his peripheral vision, he felt her watching him. "You seem pretty sure of yourself."

"Yeah, well, I guess the formidable John Michael Fortune doesn't scare me because he has no power over me."

"You say that now," said Jordana. "Just wait until he finds out you knocked up his daughter."

Tanner bit back the temptation to ask her if the reason she was so afraid of her father was because she knew he would believe keeping the baby from his—or her—father would be wrong. But he didn't want to stir the pot. Instead, he stole a sidelong glance at her. She'd wiped away the dark smudges, leaving her face nearly as fresh and makeup-free as she'd been this morning. But the light on her face exposed the depth of her exhaustion. He tightened his grip on the wheel to resist the urge to reach out a protective arm and pull her close to him.

"Yeah, well, I didn't tell him, so we will deal with that when we decide the time is right. I'm guessing it should be sooner rather than later because pretty soon your body will tell the truth for us. It's going to become pretty obvious real soon."

"Oh, so now it's *we?* Today you were so eager to take matters into your own hands, but when it comes down to dropping the bomb, then it's a *we.* I see."

Was that a sense of humor he detected?

"I'm perfectly happy to tell him myself, if that's what you want. I didn't do it today because I thought you'd want to be there when he found out."

She shrugged, a gesture that he took as a sheepish *yes.* "To be honest, until right now, I wasn't completely sure you *hadn't* told him. I'm glad you didn't. It's a catch-22. On one hand, I'm petrified to tell him, but on the other, I know it will be far worse if I don't."

"How old are you?" Tanner asked.

Out of the corner of his eye, he saw Jordana flinch. "That's a rude question."

"Well, if you're going to be my wife, I'll find out eventually. So how old?"

She shook her head again. This time, he could've sworn he'd heard her chuckle.

"Good grief, you're pretty sure of yourself, aren't you?"

He smiled. The fact that she'd quit screaming "No!" the minute he mentioned the word *marriage* was major progress.

"Actually, maybe it's more apt to say that you're full of yourself."

"Why? Because I'm not scared of your father?"

"No… Well, maybe."

"Okay, see, that's where I was going with the age thing. I wasn't trying to be rude when I asked how old you are—which, by the way, you never answered. The point I was trying to make was your dad is an alpha dog. He can sense when people are afraid of him and he plays it to his full advantage. He knows I'm not intimidated. So, the way he responds will be based on how you present the pregnancy to him."

"You're obviously not his daughter."

"Obviously. What I mean is—if we're happy and present a unified front when we tell him and your mother the news, he will handle it a lot better than if we walk in asking for his forgiveness."

As Tanner turned on his signal and prepared to make a right turn into the parking lot of a strip-mall shopping center, he caught Jordana's dubious look. But as their gazes locked, he saw something shift. Was it trust…or solidarity? It was too soon to tell, but he was getting there.

"So, where are we going?" she asked.

He pulled into a parking spot in front of Germain's Deli.

"If you're talking about right now, I'm going into the deli to get us some food for a picnic. But if you're referring to the future, that's what I wanted to talk to you about over lunch."

Seven minutes later Tanner and Jordana walked out of Germain's Deli with a feast in a bag. Included on the menu for their picnic was what Tanner promised to be the very best homemade chicken noodle soup, a loaf of fresh bread and a two-liter bottle of ginger ale. He swore the meal would zap Jordana's queasiness. To which she quipped, "My morning sickness hasn't let up in three months. If you can cure it, I will definitely marry you."

She could say that because there was no way it would happen. She'd tried every home remedy—including chicken noodle soup—and nothing had given her relief. For the sake of her child, she refused to take anything that might harm the baby. She'd simply set her mind to riding it out. It was mind over matter, really. She wasn't going to let this get the best of her. She was well aware that motherhood was not going to be easy—especially single motherhood. A little queasiness was not going to beat her.

It was in that spirit that she'd agreed to give

Tanner's miracle soup a try. One bite and she would see how it settled on her stomach.

"You're originally from Texas, right?" she asked as they headed toward a small park near her condo.

"Yep. Born and bred."

"So, how do you know about this Germain's Deli and this chicken soup? I've never even heard about it."

Tanner laughed.

"That's not surprising," he said. "It doesn't exactly strike me as the type of establishment you would frequent. The only reason I know of it is because a friend who lived here told me about it."

Jordana shrugged. He was probably right about it not being the type of place where she'd be a regular. The deli was just a little hole in the wall that had been in the same location longer than she'd been alive. The outside of the place looked worn and dated, but the inside had been clean and functional. She'd probably passed by it hundreds of times without giving it a second glance. It struck a chord in her that Tanner was adventurous enough to brave the unknown. It made her wonder how many other opportunities in life she'd overlooked or lost out on because she was stuck in her "quest for the ideal" rut.

Once they got to the park and got settled on a bench, Tanner poured ginger ale into the plastic cups the deli had supplied. He lifted his glass to hers.

"To what lies ahead. Cheers."

She touched her cup to his and took a small sip. What did lie ahead? The only thing Jordana knew for certain was that her baby would be born in September. But where would she and Tanner be this time next year? She hadn't realized until now that she'd already unconsciously conceded that Tanner would be part of the baby's life.

There was no doubt that he was a good man, and anyone who would go to the lengths he'd gone to claim his child would be a devoted father.

As he took the container of soup out of the brown paper bag and spooned up a bite for her, she felt a little ashamed for automatically assuming he would be a deadbeat who would see an illegitimate child as nothing but a burden.

He held the spoon up to her lips and she accepted the soup—the fresh-tasting broth with just the right amount of seasoning, big chunks of carrots, celery and chicken. And the noodles…to die for. They were definitely homemade; almost like dumplings.

"Wow," she said, licking drops of broth from her lips. "This is really *good.*"

Tanner beamed. "I told you."

It took a certain kind of man to sit on a public park bench and feed a woman soup—especially after the way she'd acted toward him this morning.

She blinked away the shame and decided the best way she could make up for her behavior was to simply move forward and allow him to discuss their situation with her like a rational adult.

She accepted the cardboard container and plastic spoon and took another bite of warm, savory comfort.

As she chewed, she sighed inwardly, content with the way the soup warmed her belly.

Was this pregnancy ideal? No.

Did she like the way Tanner had gone to her father to get what he wanted? *Absolutely not.*

Although, she had to admit there was something beyond Tanner Redmond's good looks that appealed to her. It was a certain strength of character that shone from the inside out. That same steadfastness she'd clung to the night of the storm.

As they sat on the bench, she didn't know if it was the food and the cool, fresh afternoon air or Tanner's easygoing company that helped her pull herself together, but she had to admit she was beginning to feel better than she had in months.

"Good soup, huh?" he asked. "How are you feeling?"

She nodded noncommittally, waiting to see how it settled in her system.

"An empty stomach can cause a lot of problems that compound on each other," he said. "Sometimes I get brand-new students who are caught up in the excitement of learning to fly and they get airsick. There's a fine line. You have to put *something* in your stomach, but it has to be the right balance of carbs and fat. Too greasy or acidic and it won't be pretty."

Jordana winced at the thought. "Stop. You're going to make me sick. My stomach was just starting to settle down."

"Fair enough." They sat in companionable silence for a moment. "What are we going to do?" she finally asked.

"I'd like you to marry me so that we can give our baby a proper family."

As Tanner's words sank in, she realized that one of the things that bothered her was that Tanner wanted to marry her. Yet, he didn't even know her. Not really. Not in the the-man-I-marry-will-know-all-about-me-and-still-love-me-despite-myself sort of way.

But her mind replayed him giving her his handkerchief—it was surprising a man's man like Tanner would even carry such a thing—and him feeding her soup and being so willing to forget today's hormonal psycho-woman display.

"So are you proposing to me?" she asked.

"I am. Are you accepting?"

Chapter Four

"Where's the ring?" Jordana asked. "It's not a proposal without a ring."

Tanner couldn't figure out if this was Jordana's way of stalling, or if she was being funny. Once he'd gotten some food in her and she'd let down her guard, she'd proven herself to have a pretty good sense of humor, but the woman did have a mind of her own.

He could tell by the look on her face there was at least a grain of seriousness to her question. He guessed he couldn't blame her. A woman like Jordana was used to the best of the best. He already sensed that the situation was less than what she'd hoped and dreamed.

Tanner's little sister was a grown woman now, and he remembered how she and her girlfriends used to chatter incessantly about weddings and bridesmaids and all sorts of girl business. He knew from listening to her and her friends that most girls had harbored fantasies of their perfect wedding since they'd been old enough to know what a wedding was.

Sitting here on the park bench, he didn't even have anything—a ring from a gumball machine or Cracker Jack box, or a pop-top or even a piece of string—that he could use as a makeshift placeholder.

"All right, I'll tell you what," he said, looking at her earnestly. "Give me twenty-four hours and I will do this right. But you have to trust me, okay?"

She opened her mouth as if to say something, but nothing came out.

"Just trust me, okay?"

Just trust me, okay?

Tanner's words echoed in Jordana's mind long after he'd dropped her off at home after their impromptu picnic in the park.

How could two simple words strike such fear in her heart?

How? From bad experience, that's how.

But Tanner Redmond had given her no reason to not trust him. In fact, he'd gone to great lengths to prove himself reliable, if not trustworthy. Jordana reminded herself of this as she stripped off her suit and got into the shower to wash away the day's strife.

She'd asked him to take her back to the office so she could get her purse and her car, but he insisted on taking her home so she could rest. He said he would arrange for the car and her purse to be delivered.

She contemplated it as she towel-dried her hair, smoothed on lotion and slid into a pair of yoga pants and an oversize T-shirt.

Not only was Tanner reliable, but he was also considerate. For some reason that's exactly what made her squirm.

She mulled it over some more as she took a box down from her closet and pulled out an old scrapbook that she'd been keeping since she was in middle school. The pink album was a little faded and some dog-eared pages stuck out from the bulging book, but the sight of it gave her a bittersweet thrill.

She'd been planning her wedding since she was twelve years old and this book was the ever-evolving blueprint to that day.

She opened the scrapbook and leafed through the pages, marveling at how her tastes really hadn't changed very much over the years. Some details—such as her ideal dress—had been updated as new designs caught her eye. She'd simply laid the photo of the most up-to-date dress on top of the older photos. It was fun to see the progression—and a little satisfying to know that for the most part, she'd known herself well enough to stick to her initial visions of her idea.

As she made her way into the kitchen with her wedding scrapbook and set the kettle on to boil water for a cup of decaffeinated tea, it struck her that Tanner fit the mold of her ideal physical *type*. But she wasn't so shallow to let that overshadow what was important…what was on the inside.

Trust me. His voice echoed in her head again.

The stakes were so high. He was asking her to give him twenty-four hours to prove to her that they should spend the rest of their lives together. This man whom she'd seen only on four separate occasions—two of which were in the same day, and the vast majority of another they'd been naked and tangled in each other's arms and conceiving a baby. Based on this history, he wanted her to throw caution to the wind and trust him with her entire future. On the few occasions when she'd leaped before she'd looked, she'd landed with a hard and regrettable thud.

She tucked the scrapbook in the crook of her arm and carried it, the steaming cup of peppermint tea and her trepidations into the living room and sat down on the couch. She started at the beginning and began flipping through the pages.

Her dream wedding…it was preserved right there on the pages of this scrapbook.

It would've been a large affair…she'd wanted everyone she knew to join in the celebration of love. Her dream dress was strapless and made of volumes of ivory satin. Actually, the shade was called *candlelight*. Surprisingly, not virginal white, only because the ivory shade went better with her hair and skin tone. The bridesmaids were in emerald-green because her dream wedding would've been in the late fall/early winter. In a church, because she was traditional like that.

If she married Tanner before the baby was showing, it would have to be a May or June wedding…spring or summer. Exactly the opposite of what she wanted.

But wasn't that just her luck with love?

She'd had three serious boyfriends in her life and each one had proven himself untrustworthy in some way. Two had cheated on her after she'd refused to sleep with them; and it became clear that the other was more interested in the Fortunes' fortune than he was in making a future with her.

Each relationship had ended badly and made her more secure in her decision to hold on to her virginity until she was certain she'd found just the perfect man.

A little voice inside her reminded her that somehow—like Arthur effortlessly extracting Excalibur from the stone—Tanner had managed to claim her V-card without the slightest resistance from her. Maybe that was a sign that he was the right man.

Then again, she'd been fooled before.

After her most recent relationship had ended— how long ago was it now…nearly three years ago—she'd even contemplated that being a virgin on her wedding night might not be such a bad choice.

That wasn't an option anymore. But marrying Tanner was.

He was a lot different than her past *mistakes*. He had his own money and had been a longtime friend of the Red Rock branch of the Fortune family. And, she had to admit, their one night together had been phenomenal. She'd heard that often a woman's first time left a lot to be desired. She'd braced herself and even half expected to be left with an *Oh, that was it?* feeling of emptiness. But Tanner had been a gentle and passionate lover.

He'd definitely left her wanting more. And if it hadn't been for the circumstances—the fear of the death and destruction they might discover out in the real world once the sun rose—things might have been different.

Plus, the kicker that had caused her guard to go up immediately was that even though they'd fallen asleep in each other's arms in the old hunting lodge where they'd sought shelter during the storm, she'd awakened alone.

Of course, Tanner hadn't abandoned her. He was out getting help to pull his Tahoe out of the ditch they'd ended up in when he'd swerved to avoid hitting a piece of debris that had blown into their path.

Her waking up alone the morning after her first time wasn't his fault. He was doing what needed to be done. And he hadn't even known she'd been a virgin. Or at least she hadn't said anything and he hadn't asked.

Still, it had been a cold, lonely morning as she'd dressed and ventured out to find him helping a

team of rescue workers hoist his truck out of the
ditch. Never before had it been clearer that she
could not entrust her happiness to anyone. Not that
she believed she'd never find someone who could
make her happy, but that she had to be the one in
charge of her own bliss.

Maybe that principle applied here, too?

Tanner was a good man. He wanted to make
them a family. Since he was providing the frame-
work of a life together, maybe she needed to be
the one who brought the love and happiness.

They had all the ingredients for a good life. So
what if their story didn't unfold like the picture-
perfect fantasy she'd created in the pages of her
scrapbook? The wedding of her dreams would
take at least six months to plan. If she and Tanner
were going to do this, she wanted to get married
before she was showing because she didn't want
her wedding march to be "Here Comes the *Pregnant* Bride."

She closed the scrapbook and took it back into
her bedroom. It was time to leave fantasy and
ideals behind. Since they were doing things out
of order anyway, maybe Tanner could learn to love
her in the end?

While Jordana was putting the book back in its
box, she heard a knock at her front door.

Her first thought was that it might be Tanner bringing her car and purse back. She left the book on the bed, quickly tugged off the sloppy T-shirt and danced out of the yoga pants. She pulled on jeans, which were already proving to be a little snug in the stomach and rear, and a loose-fitting baby-doll top that would hide her pants' tight waistband.

Knock knock knock knock—

The pounding was more insistent.

Good grief...just a minute. "Coming," she called as she threw on a long necklace to complement the outfit, but then took it off again en route to the door, not wanting to look like she'd tried too hard.

Her heart sank when she opened the door and saw not Tanner, but her mother, Virginia Fortune, standing on the porch.

"Oh, Mama. Hi." Jordana smiled, hoping her mother didn't notice the masked disappointment in her voice. Not that she wasn't always happy to see her mother, who had to be one of the sweetest women in the world...especially the way she put up with Jordana's father. A true Southern belle, Virginia was as genteel as John Michael was gruff. She was probably the only woman in the world who knew how to handle him. Or perhaps *put up with him* was a better way to put it, because John Michael Fortune took his sweet wife for granted.

"Now, what kind of a greeting is that?" Virginia asked with a good-natured grin. "Were you expecting someone else?"

That was a loaded question.

Jordana laughed and hugged her mother. "Who else might I be expecting?"

Virginia answered her with a quirk of her perfectly groomed eyebrows. "I don't rightly know."

She eyed Jordana up and down. "But you sure do look lovely tonight. Oh, and a very handsome man named Tanner Redmond asked if I would deliver your pocketbook to you. Seems you left in such a hurry with him that you left it in your office."

Virginia held out the purse. So, now Tanner had been talking to her mother?

"Come in," Jordana said. "When did you see Tanner?"

Virginia walked in and headed straight for the living room. Over her shoulder she said, "I didn't, but your daddy did. Apparently, Tanner called the office and informed Marta that you'd left your pocketbook behind. Marta gave it to me when I stopped in to see your daddy this afternoon."

Virginia made herself at home on one end of

the couch. Jordana sat on the other end, twisting her body to face her mother.

In addition to being one of the sweetest women in the world, Jordana also thought her mother had to be one of the most beautiful. Her hair, which was once a natural honey-blond, was now an elegant silver. While some Atlanta matriarchs spent a fortune trying to turn back the hands of time with Botox and expensive trips to the colorist, Virginia insisted on remaining natural. She said she'd never color her hair because she'd earned each and every strand of silver on her head. And she wore her crowning glory like a badge of honor.

Virginia leaned toward Jordana as if they were about to conspire. "So, why didn't you tell me you were seeing Tanner Redmond?"

Oh, boy. Here we go. Jordana scooted to the edge of the couch cushion and sat up straight.

"May I make you a cup of tea, Mama?" she asked, half rising, but she should've known her mother wouldn't fall for the old bait and switch.

"No, thank you, darling. Sit down. But I would love for you to answer my question."

Jordana took her time settling back into the couch cushions. "Well, I wanted to make sure the relationship was…solid before I told anyone."

Virginia's eyes sparkled. "How long have you been seeing each other?"

Jordana resisted the urge to put her hand on her belly. "Well, I guess you could say it all started the night of Wendy and Marcos's wedding. We danced."

Virginia gave a ladylike clap of her hands. "And how often does he fly in to see you?"

Jordana swallowed hard. She refused to lie to her mother. "Not nearly often enough."

Virginia swooned. "Ooh, young love. It's so beautiful. I am so happy for you, my darling."

Jordana bit her bottom lip against the urge to *hrumph*. There was no young love. There was a pregnancy out of wedlock, and the father of her child was insisting on doing the right thing.

Watching her mother beam at her, she was nearly exploding with the knowledge that Tanner was going to propose. It was so ridiculous that Virginia didn't know that Jordana knew that her mother knew—*ugh,* how long was she going to let this farce go on?

Tell her.

The need to do the right thing nudged at Jordana's insides. She'd always been able to talk to her mother. And for God's sake, she was a twenty-nine-year-old woman who was perfectly capable of taking care of herself and her baby…and the father wanted to be involved. This was not such a tragedy.

Tell her now. She can help pave the way to make breaking the news to Dad easier.

"Mama, I'm pregnant."

The dreamy smile evaporated from Virginia's face. Her hand fluttered to her neck, and her lips formed a surprised *oh*.

Jordana braced herself. "Mama, don't be mad at me, please."

Virginia blinked a couple of times then seemed to regain her composure. She reached out and took Jordana's hand with both of hers, and held it tight. The gesture was both reassuring and grounding. It seemed to help Jordana find her emotional balance.

"You are twenty-nine years old, Jordana. You're hardly a child. Why on earth would I be mad at you?" Virginia pursed her lips, an expression that ran contrary to her words. "Although, I would like to know what your plans are."

Sure, she might be nearly thirty, but where her parents were concerned, somehow she always slid back into that parent-child relationship and felt twelve years old. But her sweet, reasonable mama was right. She was a grown woman. This was her decision. Her plans…well, hers and Tanner's.

"Well, Mama, Tanner and I have been talking about getting married."

Her mother gave a single, expressionless nod. "Is that what you want?"

It could be…

"I don't know."

"Do you know he asked your father for your hand in marriage?"

Jordana nodded.

"Your father thinks he is a fine young man. He said he thinks the two of you would be well suited. That's quite an endorsement coming from John Michael Fortune. He doesn't lend his stamp of approval to many."

"Then again, he has no idea Tanner knocked up his daughter."

"Jordana, that's vulgar. You don't have to say it that way."

"But it's the truth. Daddy has no idea Tanner only wants to marry me because I'm pregnant."

The heat of humiliation crept up her neck. Saying the words aloud, acknowledging that there would be no proposal if she were not pregnant stripped away all pretense of romance and laid out the situation for what it really was.

"Well, it is the honorable thing to do. While I will not tell you what to do—because you're the only one who knows what's in your heart—I would not discourage you from marrying him. It may be the new millennium, but people still talk."

The bitter truth was hard to swallow. Even though her mother wasn't saying it, Jordana knew there was a stigma attached to the daughter of a prominent family having a baby out of wedlock. They'd been through this before with her sister Wendy when she found herself in a similar situation, pregnant with Marcos Mendoza's child. Wendy and Marcos had married and were happily living in Red Rock. Even though Jordana wholeheartedly knew she was perfectly capable of raising a child on her own, she also recognized that she was a little more traditional than she realized.

"I'm going to marry him and we are going to live in Red Rock, Texas. That's where his business is and that's where we will make our life. I can telecommute. Hopefully, if we keep the wedding modest and quiet—without a lot of hoopla— no one will keep track of our anniversary and the baby's birthday."

Virginia shook her head. "I suppose the opinions of other people should be the last thing on my mind right now. I'm sorry, honey."

"Mama, it's okay. I understand. You and I have always been able to talk so freely and openly. I want you to know how much I appreciate that." Jordana paused, trying to summon the courage to tackle the scariest issue. Really, there was no sense in beating around the bush. "How in the world am I going to tell Daddy?"

Virginia squeezed Jordana's hand. "You just leave that to me, sweetheart. Everything will be fine. However, I would like to get to know my future son-in-law, since I've only met him in passing. Why don't y'all come by the house tomorrow night for supper?"

Jordana swallowed around the hard lump that had formed in her throat. It was made of equal parts fear of what her father might do to Tanner, and gratitude that she'd been blessed with such a saint for a mother. "Are you sure Daddy is going to be okay once he knows? Tanner may have asked him for my hand, but he didn't mention the circumstances."

Virginia smiled her serene smile, the one that always seemed to surface when there was an issue she had to discuss with her husband. "Don't you worry about your daddy. He's already been through this with your sister Wendy. You just leave the rest up to me."

* * *

The Fortune estate sat on two acres of secluded land about an hour outside of Atlanta.

"Your father commutes all this way to the office every day?" Tanner asked as he steered the car along the lit winding driveway.

"Drives himself every day," Jordana said. "My brothers and sisters and I grew up in this house. It's just him and Mama now. I keep encouraging them to sell the house and move in closer to the city, but he likes the solitude. And Mama has a dream of someday seeing this house filled with grandkids. Looks like my sister Wendy and I are helping make Mama's dream come true."

He parked in the driveway and turned toward Jordana. The porch lights of the regal, two-story, Country-French-style house cast a soft glow on Jordana, highlighting just how beautiful, if not slightly nervous, she looked tonight. Pregnancy agreed with her. Or maybe he'd simply forgotten her ability to drive him mad. Her pink sweater, which hugged her in all the right places, brought out a subtle color in her cheeks and made him ache to touch her. Her blond hair hung in loose curls around her shoulders. Before he could stop, he found himself fingering a strand of it and allowing his index finger to brush the hollow of her cheek. Maybe it was his imagination, but he could've sworn she leaned into him a nearly imperceptible fraction.

"Are you okay?" he asked.

She shrugged. "Sure. Or at least I will be. I just want to get this over with."

As a former Air Force pilot, Tanner had been stuck in way tougher situations than this meeting with her folks. No disrespect to them, but this was his and Jordana's future. Not theirs.

He wasn't upset with Jordana that she'd told her parents without him. Or, as she'd said, she'd told her mother. Her mother, Virginia, was telling Jordana's father. No, it was up to Jordana how she wanted to break the news of the baby to her folks. They would tell his mom and his family together, but if this was how she wanted to handle it on her end, he supported her decision.

He and John Michael Fortune were on pretty good terms and he didn't foresee this additional piece of news changing anything. At least not on his end. A surprise *blessing,* he'd once heard an unplanned pregnancy called. If Mr. Fortune needed some time to adjust to the news, he could have his space to do so. The only thing Tanner wouldn't stand for was for him to upset Jordana. If that happened, they'd leave and the Fortunes could get in touch as soon as they were ready to play nice. But Tanner's gut feeling told him it wouldn't come to that. He just wished Jordana felt as confident as he did, because everything would be fine.

No matter what.

He moved his finger under her chin and gently tilted her head up so she would look him in the eyes.

"Don't be nervous," he whispered. "You have nothing to worry about. I'm here and I won't let him hurt you."

"He'd never hurt me. Not physically, anyway. He may be gruff, but he's not violent."

She had the most beautiful eyes, dark and almond shaped. The way their depth contrasted with her light hair gave her an exotic look that made it hard for him to take his eyes off her when she was near.

"I won't allow him to upset you, either. There's no reason to be afraid."

He touched her cheek and the poignant warmth in her eyes made him achingly aware of her. He slid his hand down and traced her lower lip with the pad of his thumb, and suddenly the atmosphere changed, the tender need was replaced by something vibrant and gripping.

A swell of suppressed desire seared through

him, gripping him by surprise. He knew he should be treading lightly, cautiously…but he just couldn't help it. He didn't want to help it.…

For a moment, they sat there transfixed in each other's gaze, and he felt protective and a little bit Neanderthal as he tried to decipher the mix of emotions playing across her face. There was a hint of fear, and trepidation. He hated that she was uncertain, he wanted her to relax, to trust him. But he also sensed that there was something more in the way she looked at him…was it desire?

Or maybe he was glimpsing his own longing reflected back at him, because he was suddenly dying to pull her into his arms and taste her lips again. He wanted to see if they were as sweet as he remembered. His gaze dropped to her mouth and the next thing he knew, he had gathered her in his arms and her lips were right there, inches from his. Then he was leaning in and kissing her.

The kiss started soft and leisurely with a brush of lips and trace of tongue. He was testing the waters, trying to gauge how receptive she would be. But holding her made his heart pound and his brain time-travel back to the night of the storm, and that was all it took for reason to fly out the window.

As if reading his mind, she slid her arms around his neck and opened her mouth, inviting him in.

He'd forgotten how all-consuming her kiss could be.

There was no wavering, no inhibition, just his mouth on hers with shades of the one night they'd spent together fueling the fire of a ferocious need for her he hadn't realized he'd harbored all these months they'd been apart. There hadn't been anyone but her since that night. And right now, in this moment, he knew in his bones there never would be anyone but Jordana from here on out.

When he turned her so that he could deepen the kiss, Jordana fisted her hands into his hair and pulled their bodies closer. His hands were on her back, and his mouth was on her lips, but his entire body responded. Every sense was heightened as if the part of him that had died on the day she left was being resuscitated by her life breath.

Why had he not realized this until now? Or maybe he simply wouldn't admit it to himself when he thought there was no possibility of a life with her.

And now there was.

As he tasted and teased, the last bit of reason he possessed took flight.

Damn.

He'd forgotten what kind of power she had over him. Most of all, he hoped here in his arms, she would finally realize she had nothing to fear. He wanted her to relax, let go and let him take charge for a while.

He heard the ragged rasp of her breath through the blood rushing in his ears. He felt the heat of her hands on his shoulders. She smelled like heaven: a sweet mix of what was probably her shampoo and a hint of something floral mingling with something soft and feminine. Yet despite the intoxicating way she smelled, the way she tasted—of sun-warmed honey and something else he couldn't quite pin down—was sexy and inviting. She nearly made him drunk with pleasure. Jordana was a seductive contradiction of vulnerability and strength, mixed with a heady sexual magnetism and a soft femininity. Everything about her teased his senses, made him hot for her and just a little bit reckless.

It had been far too long. Far too long since a woman's touch had made his blood burn with need and his body long to take her.

He was lost in the feel of her, the smell and taste of her, until something shifted and pushed its way into his awareness.

A ragged sigh escaped from him and he tightened his grip to pull her closer, but suddenly she pulled away, ducking her head and tucking a strand of hair behind her ear.

All she said was, "We can't. Not now."

She opened the car door and let herself out.

Chapter Five

"The keys to pulling off a quick wedding are extreme organization, the ability to prioritize and you must—absolutely must—be able to compromise." Virginia ticked off the advice on her fingers as Jordana helped her do the dinner dishes in the kitchen while the men were talking and enjoying a cognac in the living room.

Since Jordana couldn't drink due to the pregnancy and Virginia preferred softer drinks, mother and daughter had happily excused themselves to the kitchen to engage in a little planning while the men got to know each other better.

"Do you agree?" Virginia asked.

Jordana nodded. She was listening to her mother, but her mind kept drifting back to Tanner's kiss in the car. She put the plate she'd just finished drying in the cupboard and pressed her fingers to her lips. She'd been so nervous about facing her father that she'd been terrified that he might catch them making out in the car in the driveway like a couple of teenagers.

Now she felt ridiculous for fleeing the way she did, especially after seeing the way her father had embraced Tanner. There was no ugly scene, no shotgun behind the door. In fact, the only slightly derogatory remark her father had made was when he shook Tanner's hand and made a wisecrack about him making an honest woman out of his daughter.

And then there was the comment about him wanting the marriage to take place *sooner rather than later.* Tanner had beamed. "That's exactly what I said to her. Tomorrow night we're going to dinner to discuss our plans."

It was all going a little fast for Jordana's liking, but now that the train was in motion, it seemed futile to try and put on the brakes. Especially since her father was so onboard with the marriage.

Jordana realized given the circumstances she

had to compromise on some old expectations, but the one thing she wished she could have—even more than her dream dress—was a groom who loved her. Tanner had been wonderful; he'd been charming and patient, but the fact remained that this was a marriage of convenience, a union in name only. Jordana couldn't help but wonder what would become of them once their child was grown and set out to make his or her own life.

That was something they needed to discuss before they made anything official. Before they said "I do" and were stuck, they needed to make sure they were both on the same page.

Stuck...the thought made her want to run.

As she dried another piece of her mother's china—Wedgwood Black Astbury pattern, it had been their family's special-occasion china for as far back as Jordana could remember, and her mother had taken it out for tonight's dinner—and she handled the piece with deliberate care, she wondered if her mother ever felt *stuck*. Her father wasn't an easy man to live with and ninety-nine-point-nine percent of the time he was more focused on work than he was on her or the family. It was almost as if they were partners in the business of marriage. Mama was CEO and lone employee of the home-and-family division of the Atlanta

Fortunes. Daddy was always preoccupied with everything but her.

Even though her mother was a good sport—in fine Southern tradition they never aired their dirty laundry—didn't she ever get lonely?

The notion made Jordana panic at the thought of roping herself into a situation where she might find herself divorced after their child was grown and independent. Or worse yet…stuck in an empty shell of a relationship.

She shuddered.

"Are you okay?" Virginia asked. "You seem a million miles away."

Jordana gently set down the plate.

"You and Daddy have been married for thirty-seven years. I know it hasn't been easy." She turned and faced her mother head-on. "How have you made it work? Weren't there ever times you wanted to give up and leave?"

Virginia turned off the water she'd been running to rinse the stemware. She dried her hands on a dish towel and took off her apron. "Honey, let's sit down."

She motioned toward the kitchen table and Jordana followed.

"Marriage is an interesting arrangement. It's part thrill ride, but mostly cross-country marathon. The butterflies and fireworks wear off far too soon and what you're left with is the quality of the person you married and how you connect. Each couple is different. So, what works for your daddy and me may not necessarily work for you and Tanner. But if you both honor your vows to put your family and your marriage first, someday your daughter will be looking in awe at your long-lasting marriage. You'll be soothing her fears about how to make marriage last."

One thing Jordana could say was that she and Tanner had no problem *connecting*. She thought about his kiss earlier and how she'd pulled away. She wished she could go back and do it over. Easy to say now that Tanner had been heartily welcomed into the family. At least they'd cleared that hurdle. Now she needed to realign her expectations. She'd always been the good girl, the rule follower. Wendy was the wild daughter—so really the news of her pregnancy was not so surprising. Emily was the beauty, and Jordana was the smart one—the sister who should've been too smart to find herself in this situation.

Now, the challenge was to use her head to ensure this marriage lasted.

Tanner would've been lying if he hadn't admitted that he'd been a little nervous joining the

Fortunes for dinner tonight. However, he knew everything would work out fine in the end, because the only thing he wanted from John Michael Fortune was his blessing to marry his daughter, which he had granted yesterday afternoon.

Tonight had been strictly for Jordana's benefit because full disclosure was so important to her. Not that Tanner wanted to keep secrets from his future family members, but frankly, his life with Jordana after they were married was private business.

Besides, he sensed John Michael Fortune was a man who respected strength. Strength meant not asking for approval on how to run his life. Tanner knew the type of man he would want his own daughter to marry would be one with a confident plan.

He was thirty-three years old. Business was good at Redmond Flight School. He had a solid future, and while getting married and having a baby hadn't been part of his immediate plan, it was now. That was another area where he sensed that he and Mr. Fortune were alike. They both were successful in their respective businesses because they were able to proactively adapt to change.

Jordana was quiet in the seat next to him on the

way home from her parents' house. "It was a nice night," he said, trying to gauge her mood.

"It was," she agreed. "I didn't quite know how my father would take the news. He must like you. That's a good thing."

"What's not to love?" Tanner teased, slanting her a sidelong glance and a wide grin to show he was kidding. She looked tired, but there was a lighter air about her now than when they'd first arrived.

"What's *not* to love?" she repeated. "According to my father you're golden. He's obviously a fan. Isn't that all that matters?"

He liked this feisty side of her.

"No, other things matter, too."

"Oh, yeah?" she asked. "Like what?"

"You, obviously. Your happiness. The baby. Shall I continue?"

He glanced at her, and for a moment his gaze dropped to her full bottom lip. He'd been stupid to kiss her earlier, despite how badly he'd wanted her. Something had come over him. Well, yeah, she obviously had that effect on him.

But tonight made him realize that no matter how attracted he was to her, she might need some time to warm up to their new life together. He would not push himself on her physically. He would wait until she was absolutely ready.

And he knew she would be worth the wait.

"That's very sweet," she said. "But, I was thinking about something tonight. Are you *sure* you want this marriage?"

"Are you having second thoughts?"

She sighed. "Tanner, my parents have been married for thirty-seven years. In my family we don't take marriage lightly. It's not something we do for the short-term. My parents have always taken their vows seriously and I want the same thing."

He tightened his grip on the wheel, not quite sure where she was going with this. "Your dad and I had a similar conversation."

"You did?"

Tanner nodded, but he kept his eyes on the road. "We did. He said basically the same thing that you just said. I told him I'm taking this serious, too. I came from a broken home and I know the kind of hell divorce puts kids through. I don't want that for my kid. I want my child to have a traditonal family with all the emotional advantages a mother and father who live together provide. Why do you think I've been so persistent?"

She was quiet and he glanced over at her to try

and read her expression, but she was staring at her fingernails, picking at her nail polish. Her hair had fallen forward over her shoulder and was casting shadows on her face.

"What are you thinking?" he asked.

She put her hands in her lap. "I'm thinking that neither one of us knows what the future holds. So, I'm thinking if we're going to do this…if we're going to get married, we need to have some rules. I know you don't love me—"

Love her? It had been so long since he'd contemplated the possibility of being in love that he didn't even know if he remembered what love was.

She continued, "I can't make a life with someone unless we can guarantee that we're going to be exclusive. Otherwise, it would just be too hard— especially if we're going to live together like man and wife and raise a family together."

Hmm… He hadn't even thought about that. Truth was he'd been so wrapped up in the flight school, he hadn't had time to date. Come to think of it, he couldn't remember the last woman— before Jordana—who'd affected him like she did.

"I'm fine with that. In fact, it's kind of a no-brainer. We honor our marriage, our marriage vows. I don't think I could live any other way. Does that make you feel better?"

He heard her sharp intake of breath, as if she wanted to say something else, but had stopped.

"Talk to me," he said. "One of my nonnegotiables is you have to promise me complete honesty. I'm not a mind reader." He hadn't meant for that to come out sounding so harsh. So, he tempered it with, "The only way I'm going to know what you want is if you tell me, okay?"

She nodded. "Okay, then the other thing is… since we barely know each other, I think we need to allow each other an escape clause."

"What do you mean?" A gamut of perplexing emotions flooded through him. One minute she was talking about being true and how hard her parents had worked at making their marriage work, now she was negotiating an *escape clause?*

"What I mean is we hardly know each other and we're talking about taking a step that people who have known each other for years agonize over. Think about it…what if we get married and we end up being incompatible?"

Honey, you and I are way too compatible. That's what got us into this situation. He almost had to bite his tongue to keep himself from speaking his thoughts, because he didn't want to pressure her or make her uncomfortable.

So instead, he said, "I'm not sure I follow you."

"What I'm saying, plain and simple, is if we get married and in the first year one of us feels as if the situation isn't working—for any reason—that person is free to walk away."

A disposable marriage? Those were the first words that came to mind as he tried to digest her suggestion. The next thoughts felt like someone had dropped a heavy weight in his gut: Was this the approach his father had taken when it came to marriage and family? Obviously, he'd stuck around long enough to father three kids, but not long after his little sister was born, their father was long gone. Tanner hadn't heard from him or anything of him in a good twenty years.

"I don't know, Jordana. That makes it sound way too easy to just walk away."

"Well, my thought is if one of us finds the marriage so unpalatable—in the first year… I'm not suggesting we keep this escape clause active forever. Only the first year. And if one of us finds it impossible to stay in that first year, then they should be free to go."

Tanner was shaking his head before he even realized what he was doing.

"An unhappy home is no place to raise a child," Jordana said.

Tanner flipped on his blinker and checked traffic before merging into the right lane to take the exit that led to Jordana's condo. He flipped on his left blinker and stopped at the red traffic light at the bottom of the off-ramp.

While he waited for the signal to change he turned and faced her. "All I'm saying is I think that makes it way too easy to walk away without trying."

"Tanner, I can guarantee you that if I marry you I'm going to do everything in my power to make this marriage work—"

"And I am, too. So I really don't understand why this escape clause is such a big deal." He was raising his voice again, and he took a deep breath to calm himself down.

She blinked at him for a moment, looking a little stunned.

Finally, she said, "I think this is the perfect example of why we need it. If we're at a stalemate over this and we're not even married…that doesn't bode well at all. I won't marry you unless you grant me that provision."

The light turned green and Tanner drove the car through the intersection without answering her. Jordana could see the ticking in his jaw and she knew he wasn't happy with her stipulation.

She wasn't trying to be defeatist or approach this marriage like it was doomed before it even started. She just wanted a little insurance.

"You know," she said, "you could look at it from the standpoint that having an escape clause might make us work even harder to make things right. That way, there would be no reason for one of us to exercise that option."

He was quiet as he drove and she couldn't tell if he was thinking or ignoring her. So, she honored his silence and rode the rest of the way without saying anything else. She could only hope that he didn't mistake her silence for wavering on her stance. Without his agreement, there would be no wedding.

This was the deal breaker, and if he couldn't give her this, then they probably wouldn't be able to live together, anyway.

Her sorrow at the thought of this formed a big painful knot in her chest. She rested her hands on her stomach, reinforcing that she was doing the right thing, despite the thought of how close she'd been to having Tanner, but instead, ending up alone…again.

When the knot loosened and dissipated, she was surprised by how empty she felt.

A few minutes later, Tanner steered the car into

the spot in front of Jordana's condo. Unsure of where they stood, she decided to give him tonight to think about things. He hadn't officially proposed yet. He'd had a lot thrown on him tonight— a huge dose of the reality of what it would be like to involve himself with the Fortunes.

If nothing else, it underscored that they weren't an easy clan to assimilate into.

Maybe tonight had scared him off…well, she'd know soon enough.

"Good night, Tanner. Thank you for being a good sport about the dinner with my parents. No matter what happens between us, you'll be at least an indirect member of this family since you'll be actively involved in our baby's life. I know you have a lot to think about. So, I'll leave you to do just that."

She pulled her keys from her purse and started to open the car door.

"Jordana, please wait." Tanner's hand gently held on to her arm. "I know you're tired, but I want to make sure we're clear on a couple of things before we say good-night."

Jordana let go of the door handle and settled back into the car seat. He was right, she was bone tired, but knowing she might have a clearer understanding of where her future stood—what *their* future held—made her adrenaline rush.

Ever familiar with the negotiating philosophy of *He who speaks first gives away the position of power,* she sat there quietly waiting for Tanner to say what was on his mind.

She remembered how he'd kissed her earlier and how she'd fouled that up by pulling away. Regret hung over her like a shadow.

She wanted a do-over, but if their kiss in her parents' driveway had been bad timing, now—as they negotiated their future—would be ridiculous. He was such a good-looking guy. A great guy who could have his choice of women, she was sure. Here she was, looking at their coming together as a *negotiation.* Not very romantic. The problem was, she could see the errors in hindsight, but she didn't have enough experience to stop herself before she made the faux pas.

If this were business, instincts would guide her. But in matters of love she didn't have a clue.

So what did he see in her? She wasn't beautiful like her sisters. They got the looks; she got the brains. Well, Emily had gotten her fair share of both, but while her sisters were comfortable in their own skin, Jordana had always been more confident in her aptitude. Books and grades were something she could control. The human heart, however, was fickle and flighty. And unreliable. Especially hers. One minute it told her to do one thing—to not kiss Tanner in her parents' driveway—then the next minute it was telling her she'd made a mistake. She hated this uncertainty. Frankly, she was only trying to protect herself from getting hurt.

Tanner cleared his throat. "I've been thinking about what you said a few minutes ago. Are you afraid you won't be able to stick it out in this marriage? Because for me, it's a no-brainer."

A no-brainer?

He must have seen the question in her eyes. "What I mean is, when I say 'til death do us part, I will mean it."

There was so much conviction in his voice, in his face. She wanted to believe him.

"But the more I thought about it," he continued, "the more I realized I can't force you to stay if your heart's not in it."

Now he was talking about hearts... Her stomach did an odd swoop and drop.

"So, I'll give you your two nonnegotiables if you'll give me one."

Jordana nodded to indicate she was listening, hoping against hope that what he was about to say wouldn't be the final straw that would end them in a stalemate.

"A little matter came up this evening when I was talking to your father. I wanted to discuss it with you before he mentioned it. Obviously, one of us will have to relocate. Since my business is established in Red Rock, I was hoping you'd be willing to move. Your father said he would be willing to let you telecommute."

That was his nonnegotiable? Jordana bit the inside of her cheek to keep herself from smiling. Another hard, fast business principle was to keep a poker face—especially when you were getting exactly what you wanted. Yesterday's conversation with her mother replayed in her head. To make matters less socially awkward, she and her mother had agreed on a quiet, simple wedding and Jordana's relocating to Red Rock to have the baby. But Tanner didn't need to know that.

"I know I mentioned it briefly when I first arrived, but at that point we hadn't even established that I'd be an active part of the baby's life. I just want to make sure you were onboard with moving. Since you weren't a fan of me going to your father to ask for your hand, I wanted you to know this came up tonight. I didn't want you to misconstrue the conversation I had with him tonight."

"So, let me get this straight," she said. "If I agree to move to Red Rock, you'll agree to monogamy and the escape clause?"

"Yes, that's right."

Rule number three was never give in too easily.

"Well, given that you haven't formally proposed yet—" she held up her naked left hand and wiggled her fingers "—I'll think about it and give you my answer once you do."

She knew she was being a bitch, and it was all she could do to force the words out. Her heart was pounding, as if kicking her for not leaning into him and kissing him and saying, *Yes! Of course! That's exactly what I want.*

But her head was insisting if she didn't make it easy on him, maybe he would decide this arrangement was too much trouble and change his mind now.

Better to lose him now than after she'd lost her heart to him.

As it stood, she was already three-quarters of the way gone.

Chapter Six

At seven o'clock the next morning, Tanner's cell phone rang as he was getting ready to leave his hotel room to get breakfast. John Michael Fortune was on the line, informing him that he and his wife had further discussed Tanner and Jordana's predicament and they had agreed that it would be best if Tanner and Jordana were married before she left Atlanta and moved away to Red Rock.

"My concern isn't that you won't do the right thing by my daughter. It's just the opposite. I'm afraid that Jordana might get cold feet if you didn't make an honest woman out of her while you have the chance."

Tanner tossed his keys on the table by the door and sat on the edge of the bed, unsure where John Michael was heading with this conversation and hating the uncertainty that all this talk about trust had sparked. Tanner's father hadn't been trustworthy, hadn't kept his promise to his own family. No. Being a dirtbag and running when the going got tough wasn't a gene passed down in the DNA. Staying and keeping promises was a choice, not an inevitable part of one's biological makeup.

If Fortune believed in him, he had to believe in himself.

Tanner cleared his throat.

"You trust me, but you don't trust your own daughter?"

Fortune harrumphed. "She's quiet and level-headed most of the time. But she has a stubborn streak stronger than the stink of a skunk on an old coon dog."

Tanner chuckled at the dry way Fortune had ground out the colloquialism. But a few seconds later he was sobered by the thought that he had already glimpsed that side of her. It had been harder than roping a wild steer when it came to pinning down Jordana about the baby; and then there was the case of her not bending an inch when it came to that damn *escape clause* she'd insisted on before she would agree to marry him.

He'd been so concerned about making sure he didn't follow in his old man's footsteps, he hadn't really considered the possibility of her running away. However, until they said *I do* he supposed there was always the chance that she might. Of course, there was the possibility that she might run after they were married, too, but it would be a lot more difficult to leave once the marriage was signed and sealed.

"Nah, we've talked and I'm not worried about her changing her mind. So, I think we're good. All that's left is she wants a traditional proposal. So, no need to worry."

Not to mention, he planned on making Jordana and their child so happy that she would never feel the need to exercise that option. He would make sure he gave his child the kind of home his father never cared enough to give him and his siblings.

"Good," said John Michael. "I'm glad you're so confident. Even so, I think we need a little insurance policy. There's a place about seventy miles outside of Atlanta. It's called Château Enchantée. I want you to take my daughter to the resort for a couple of nights, have dinner, formally propose to her like she wants and then you can get married the following evening. My wife will arrange all the details of the wedding for you so all you'll need to do is show up."

Sounded like everything already had been arranged. Tanner gritted his teeth and wondered if his future in-laws would try to run their lives once he and Jordana were in Red Rock.

"It'll be a surprise for Jordana. You're both busy. You have a lot on your plates with work, the move and the baby on the way. As I said, frankly, we would prefer that you tied the knot sooner rather than later. And we intend to make sure things are as easy as possible for you to do that."

In other words, they were arranging this to ensure it got done how and when Mama and Papa Fortune wanted it. Tanner was becoming an expert at deciphering John Michael Fortune–speak. He was also learning that the man didn't take no for an answer. Tanner wondered how the man was going to react once some firm boundaries were erected.

"I don't know about this—" But Fortune obviously hadn't heard him because he put Virginia on the phone, or maybe he thought he could wear Tanner down by tag teaming him.

"Tanner?" Her Southern accent made his name sound like *Tanna*. "Hi, honey, I just wanted to let you know that the wedding will happen right there at Château Enchantée. Does that sound good to you?"

"I'm not sure," he said. "I don't know anything about this place. Is it something Jordana would choose?"

"Trust me, hon, it will be fine."

Cradling the phone between his ear and his shoulder, he moved from the bed to the desk and did an internet search where he discovered this Château Enchantée joint was an Americanized knockoff of a French castle. They specialized in "storybook weddings," or so the website proclaimed.

The words *cookie cutter* and *prefabbed* seemed an apt substitute for storybook, but he kept the thought to himself as Virginia carried on about various restaurants in the resort where he could make a reservation for the proposal dinner and how she thought it would be best to book two rooms for the night before the ceremony—one for each of them. "Because you know how people love to talk. Now, what y'all do once you get there is your own business. I don't want to know." Her laugh sounded nervous.

He supposed the Fortune name carried as big a punch in the Atlanta area as it did in Texas. Growing up dirt poor, he'd never had to worry about people being interested in his business. However, since the Fortunes were so prominent in the southeast, Virginia had a valid point. Probably the reason they were arranging the wedding outside of Atlanta. A place like Château Enchantée that specialized in weddings would be discreet.

Plus, he didn't want to force himself on Jordana by presuming she would want to share a bed. Not that he didn't want her. He did in the worst way. But he wanted her to come to him as spontaneously as she had that night of the storm. The night that had brought them to this juncture in the road.

"It will be a small ceremony," Virginia said. "My husband and I will probably be the only witnesses since all of Jordana's siblings are in Red Rock, and it's such short notice. Well, and we just want this to be a nice, quiet affair. You understand, don't you? Once word gets out in Atlanta, then everyone will know."

She sighed, but not long enough for Tanner to get a word in.

"The ceremony will be followed by a family dinner," she said. "Oh! And, of course, you're more than welcome to fly in your folks if you'd like."

His folks? His mother, sister and brother. He wondered if the Fortunes would think he was quite so acceptable for their daughter if they knew the circumstances under which he'd grown up.

The suggestion to invite his family was clearly an afterthought, but everything had been moving so fast, he hadn't even had a chance to think about telling his family that he was getting married and would soon be a father.

"With all due respect, Mrs. Fortune, how do you think your daughter will take this…this surprise wedding? Don't women usually plan for months and have very specific things in mind for their day?" He wanted to say, *You know her better than I do.* But at that particular moment, he wondered if that was true.

For a moment, Virginia Fortune didn't answer him and he wondered if he'd offended her. "Given your circumstances, you don't have the luxury of taking months to plan a wedding."

He sat down on the edge of the bed.

"As much as I appreciate your help with this, I have to tell you up front, I'm not going to force Jordana into anything she doesn't want. If she feels ambushed or needs a little time or has a different vision for our wedding, I'll have to honor her wishes."

Virginia laughed. "Well, you know how she is. She might not like it at first, but honey, there's a reason she's twenty-nine and still single. She gets cold feet awfully easily. Sometimes, she just needs a little nudge to help her make up her mind. Oh, wait just a minute. My husband wants to say something to you."

Tanner raked his free hand through his hair. Couldn't they sense what he sensed? That there was probably a reason Jordana ran away from relationships. Tanner had a sneaking suspicion that somewhere along the line she'd been hurt badly. What else would make her so gun shy? Maybe her stubborn streak developed as she tried to live her own life—free from her parents' control. Either way, Tanner's gut was telling him that backing her into a corner wasn't going to help build her trust.

"Son, let me offer you a valuable piece of advice that's going to come in handy in the years ahead." John Michael was back on the line. "Sometimes you're going to have to help Jordana realize what she wants and what she needs may be two very different things. I would suggest you start with this particular situation and take the upper hand from the get-go. Otherwise, she's going to lead you on a merry chase. Her mother and I want this wedding to happen quickly and quietly. You're going to get married at Château Enchantée. Then we will be there to help celebrate the wedding with you. Then you and Jordana will go to Red Rock to live and have the baby. Do you understand me?"

Fortune didn't give Tanner a chance to respond before he'd hung up the phone, leaving the rhetorical question hanging in the air.

Later that night, Tanner waited for Jordana to join him for dinner at Tyler's on the Twenty-Seventh, a restaurant on the top floor of one of the downtown Atlanta high-rises. He'd wanted to pick her up, but she insisted on meeting him there because she had to work late.

Their intimate table for two was next to a large window and he stared out at the impressionistic rendering of the skyline at sunset. The evening was beginning its amber, salmon and turquoise light show. It was a picture-perfect backdrop to set the stage for what he hoped would be a perfect night.

Or at least as perfect as it could be given what he was about to do. He fingered the jeweler's box in his right jacket pocket, reassuring himself he was doing the right thing.

He wasn't questioning the proposal, which would happen at dessert. After their entrée was served, Tanner would excuse himself from the table and give the waiter the ring. The waiter would put the ring on a platter and "serve it" for dessert.

He had no doubt that he wanted to marry Jordana. He would do right by his child. His concern lay in the matter of whether he was doing the right thing by tipping her off to her parents' *grand surprise*.

It was black-and-white that he wouldn't let them dictate how and when he proposed. That was a no-brainer. The matter of them barging in and taking over the wedding, however, was another story.

In business, John Michael Fortune had a reputation for getting what he wanted. But this wasn't business. This was his and Jordana's life. His instincts told him that he'd better set the tone now or his in-laws would expect they could play puppeteer in his and Jordana's marriage. Since he fully intended to honor his *'til death do us part* vow, he had no intention of letting someone else run their lives…for the rest of their lives.

Granted, he was still getting to know his bride-to-be, but he had a gut feeling that she would feel

ambushed by this controlling *surprise*. That was
no way to begin a life together.

So, tonight he would propose and then he would
carefully present the option of getting married at
Château Enchantée. If she was game for this impromptu wedding, he was, too. He'd driven out
there today to check it out. There was no denying
the place was classy with its marble floors, high,
arched ceilings with columns and gigantic fresh
flower arrangements everywhere. Of course it was
classy. Virginia wouldn't let her daughter settle
for anything less. And from the looks of things
it was probably very expensive, too. Especially
given that Virginia and the staff at Château Enchantée would be able to pull everything together
in two days. They'd even arranged for Jordana
to sign the marriage license right before the ceremony—but since he was telling her, they could
go to the courthouse and get it themselves. They'd
covered every minute detail, and he hoped if it
wasn't what Jordana wanted, the Fortunes could
stop this monster snowball and get a refund. If she
wasn't into it, he'd be the one to deal with her parents. Hell, he'd even reimburse them any expenses
they'd incurred. All he wanted was for her to be
happy.

Tanner sensed Jordana before he saw her. Her

presence pulled him out of his dark thoughts. Their gazes snared and she smiled at him as she closed the space between them in the restaurant. She looked beautiful with her blond hair curled loosely around her shoulders. Her blue dress with its low-cut neckline showcasing her assets to their best advantages. He wondered if she'd changed clothes before dinner or if she'd worn that sexy dress to work.

Damn, she was gorgeous. He was one lucky guy.

His thoughts raced to their one night together and it gave him a rush that zapped him straight in the gut and ignited into a smoldering burn before it traveled south. He gave his head a quick shake to make the erotic thoughts scatter.

Jordana was carrying his child. She was going to be his wife.

His wife.

They would be a family.

He needed to treat her with due respect. That was enough to pull him back into line.

One last time, he fingered the jeweler's box in his pocket, as if confirming it was still there. The bulk of it reassured him as he stood to greet her.

"You look beautiful." He smiled and took her hand, dusting it with a light kiss.

"You clean up pretty well yourself," she said as she lowered herself onto the chair he'd pulled out for her.

After he sat down, he gazed at Jordana across the table. The soft light cascading in through the windows bathed her clear skin and her fine features in a soft pink glow. He took a moment to drink in her beauty.

This woman had grown up with the best. It was a daunting fact, but Tanner resolved right there at that moment that he wouldn't disappoint her.

"Are you hungry?" he asked.

"Actually, I am. I've been running nonstop all day."

There was an easy flow of conversation between them as they talked about how they'd spent their days. She'd been in meetings all day. "I won't bore you with the details. What did you do?"

Now wasn't the time to get into that because it would inevitably lead to a conversation about what her parents had in store and he wanted to save that for later, after she'd accepted the ring.

"I did some sightseeing." It sounded thin and the way she looked at him confirmed as much.

"Really? I didn't take you for the sightseeing type."

"What does that mean?"

"I don't know..." She shrugged. "I guess you seem sort of business focused. Like the sort that wouldn't take time away from work to see the sights even though your business is in Texas and you're here."

So that was how she saw him. Actually, she had him pegged.

"I know how to have fun," he countered. "I can balance work and my personal life."

"When was the last time you had a date?"

The question threw him. Here he was with a two-carat ring in his pocket, ready to ask the woman to spend the rest of her life with him, and she was asking about his dating life.

"Not since you were in Red Rock."

She squinted at him, looking as if she were trying to figure out whether he was trying to play her or not.

"You didn't take me out on a date when I was in Red Rock. We danced at my sister's wedding and then we..."

She looked down at her hands as her voice trailed off. A flush of pink colored her cheeks.

"Well, then here's to first dates." He reached for his wine goblet. "We need something to drink. We can't toast with empty glasses."

He motioned the waiter over. He and Jordana

argued a little when Tanner refused the wine list and ordered a bottle of French sparkling water and two champagne glasses.

"Just because I'm not drinking doesn't mean you have to abstain."

"There's nothing worse than watching another person get sloppy when you're completely sober."

"I'm not suggesting you drink an entire bottle. But please go ahead if you'd like to have a glass with dinner."

The woman knew her own mind and wasn't afraid to speak it. It was one of the many things he loved about her—

Loved?

His mouth went dry and suddenly it was way too warm in the room. As he removed his jacket, it occurred to him that he'd never used the word *loved* in the same sentence when he was talking about qualities he admired in a woman—then again, he'd never proposed to a woman before.

Tanner seemed a little subdued tonight, Jordana thought as the waiter refilled their water glasses and cleared their place settings. Maybe he was having second thoughts?

As he excused himself from the table, an odd twinge of emotion constricted her heart. She couldn't quite put her finger on the feeling. Was it disappointment or...what?

It certainly wasn't relief. She didn't want him to have second thoughts. She wanted him to fall in love with her.

The realization was so ridiculous that she immediately swept it from her mind. It was too late for romance. He'd never spoken of love or passion or even wanting to see what *they* could be together. Their situation was closer to a business merger than it was a romantic union of the souls. The quicker she got that through her head, the better off she'd be.

She traced the rim of her water glass, hating the uncertainty. One minute, she was sure that marrying him was the right thing to do—the right thing for the baby. But when she sensed a shift in Tanner's mood, in the span of a heartbeat, she questioned everything.

He was back sooner than she thought he would be, and she smiled so he wouldn't see her anxiety.

"How about some coffee?" he asked.

"Decaf tea would be nice."

He raised his hand to signal the waiter, who appeared with a tray that was covered by a silver dome.

"The dessert you ordered, sir." The server set the covered plate in front of Jordana.

She looked at Tanner. "Oh, no, thank you. Nothing else for me. I couldn't eat another bite."

He smiled. "I think you'll like this."

Something in the way he was looking at her made her stomach swoop in a figure eight that made her hopeful again.

Tanner nodded and the waiter pulled away the dome with a flourish. On a plate where the pastry should've been was a small light blue box.

A Tiffany box—

Jordana opened her mouth to speak, but no sound came out. Her voice was stopped up by several dozen conflicting emotions knotted together and lodged in her throat.

She shouldn't have been surprised by this. She knew it was coming, but she hadn't really expected it tonight. But why not tonight?

Because the whole situation still seemed completely unreal.

Then, Tanner was down on one knee in front of her with the ring box in his hand.

"Jordana, will you marry me?"

Chapter Seven

Maybe there was hope for the two of them after all, Jordana thought as she strapped herself into Tanner's plane. They were flying to Red Rock today—just two days after she'd accepted his proposal. Everyone in the restaurant had broken into applause after she'd said yes and Tanner had pulled her up into a hug, planting a kiss on her lips and spinning her around so that her feet actually lifted off the ground.

To the uninformed, they probably appeared to be very much in love—the beautiful two-carat traditional round diamond, which was so brilliant it was blinding, made a believable prop. So much so that she'd actually convinced herself that maybe, just maybe all the effort he'd put into making the proposal special and telling her parents that as much as they appreciated their kindness, the two of them wanted to wait until they got back to Red Rock and she got settled in before they rushed through a wedding ceremony.

Even though she knew she wouldn't have the wedding she'd always dreamed about—the one that was detailed in her scrapbook—she wanted to do things as *right* as possible. Because despite the fact that the circumstance dictated that she let go of a lot of her ideals, she was entering into this marriage with the firm hope that she would get married one time and stay married to the father of her child.

That meant she would have one wedding. She wanted to make it as close to perfect as possible. She loved her mother, but she didn't want to walk down the aisle to her mother's version of good enough.

Her father was not happy. But Tanner had handled him. Really, for the first time in her life she realized if she went against her father's wishes, there really wasn't a whole lot he could do.

So she and Tanner had left. He, with a confident

swagger; she, with a leave of absence from her job at Fortune South and a heavy heart, but also with a seed of hope in her core.

Of course everything would be for naught if this oversize tin can crashed between Atlanta and Red Rock.

No! Stop thinking about that.

She blinked away the morbid thoughts, and trained her gaze on Tanner, who was doing a final instrument check before they took off. She studied his handsome profile and refocused on all the blessings in her life.

She had the Rock of Gibraltar on her left ring finger, given to her by a man who she could love... really, she could...there was hope for that...and she was pregnant with his child.

A lot of blessings. A lot to be grateful for. Those happy thoughts were a good distraction from how much she hated to fly.

Tanner caught her staring and smiled. "You ready to go?"

She nodded, probably a little unconvincingly, because he asked, "Are you okay?"

"No, I am. I'm fine. I just hate to fly."

"Why do you hate to fly? Don't be scared. It's safer than traveling by car."

She shrugged and her hand found its way to her

belly, a protective gesture that had become second nature lately.

"I get airsick," she said.

"I know you can't take anything for the motion sickness right now, but do you usually take something to take the edge off?"

"Usually not. Dramamine makes me loopy and I hate that feeling almost as much as feeling sick. But even though I don't like to fly, I do realize it's the most logical way to travel—especially for business. So, I suck it up."

"Never fear," he said. "You're in good hands here. It should be a smooth flight because we have good weather today."

She was in good hands, she reminded herself as Tanner steered the plane down the runway. In more ways than one her entire future depended on him. She had no choice but to trust that her entire future as Mrs. Tanner Redmond wouldn't be as bleak as she'd first feared.

As the plane lifted off the ground, for the first time in her life she wasn't praying for the aircraft to remain airborne. Instead, her heart was hoping that this marriage of convenience would take root and grow into something steadfast and strong.

"Look, right down there." As he prepared for the final approach to the airport, Tanner gestured to a large spread of property bordered by white three-rail fencing. From fifteen-hundred feet in the air, it looked like a green, brown and white square in a patchwork quilt. But to Tanner, it was home.

"See that?" He felt like a giddy kid.

Jordana nodded.

"That's home. All sixteen acres of it."

"It looks…lovely," she said. "At least what I can see of it from all the way up here does."

Tanner laughed. "I'll give you the grand tour once we get there."

The noise of the plane's engine made it difficult for them to talk. Instead of trying to verbalize further thoughts, he summed up what he was thinking with a thumbs-up.

He was proud of his spread and eager for Jordana to settle in and make herself at home. There was plenty of room for her and the baby—in fact, more room than he'd needed living there alone. But the property had come available at just the right time—just as business at the flight school had taken off and he was feeling financially secure and tired of throwing away his money on rent. He'd been thinking ahead when he purchased it. It was a place where he'd wanted to raise a family. He just hadn't realized it would happen so soon. And while he was glad she'd come home with him, he realized as they flew over the ranch that he'd left out of Red Rock in such a furious hurry on a mission to track her down that he hadn't given much thought to the logistics of bringing her back and what would happen once he got her home.

He stole a quick glance at Jordana, admiring her profile, the delicate curve of her jawline, the sweep of her neck, the swell of her breasts. The mere sight of her sitting next to him stirred longing that was all consuming.

He remembered the ardent passion with which they'd made love that night of the storm, and he knew that it would be hard to control himself if they shared a bed.

Could lovemaking that intense hurt the baby? He didn't want to take a chance.

For the sake of his child, they should probably have separate bedrooms—at least at first, until Jordana settled in and the baby was born. He had to take things slow, allow her time to adjust and get used to their new life. Since she hadn't exactly jumped into this marriage enthusiastically, Tanner knew, despite how much he desired her, he'd better keep his distance, at least for a while.

Tanner's ranch was a scenic, twenty-minute drive from the airport. Jordana wasn't sure what she'd been expecting or what she'd envisioned when she pictured Tanner in his natural habitat, but it wasn't the sprawling, Spanish-style hacienda where they ended up once they were safely on the ground in Red Rock, Texas.

The plot of land he'd pointed out from the air did not do the property justice. It was a lot more house than a bachelor needed—four bedrooms and four baths, she discovered as he gave her the grand tour.

He started on the far side of the house, showing her three spare bedrooms—one, which he'd set up as an office. The other two were set up to accommodate guests. The two guest rooms had en suite bathrooms. A third bath was off the hall near the open, spacious family room–kitchen, where they ended up.

Jordana glanced around the large rooms, taking in the framed, aviation-themed, black-and-white photos hung in groupings on the white walls. The overall feeling to the decor was masculine and it very much reflected Tanner's essence. On closer observation, she noticed many of the 8x10s were of Tanner, and what she guessed was Redmond Flight School and various aspects of his career. She walked up for a closer look. Some of the pictures featured him with other people—smiling from the cockpit of a plane, doing a grip-and-grin as he presented a certificate to what she presumed was a flight-school graduate, standing next to the Redmond Flight School sign, giving a thumbs-up and mugging for the camera. Other photos were of him in his Air Force uniform, standing with two colleagues presenting a flag, arm-in-arm with four men wearing identical camouflage in an aircraft hangar with a huge plane in the background.

"These are great photos," she said, moving in for a closer look at one of a soldier in full camouflage gear and a child in what looked like a war-torn Middle Eastern city. It was a profile shot and he was wearing a helmet, but it looked like him.

"Is this you?" Tanner nodded and seemed to straighten with pride.

"Where was it taken?"

"Over in Iraq when I was in the Air Force."

"You were in Iraq?" How did she not know this about him?

"Sure was. That was 2003."

It was nine years ago. He'd been twenty-four. She couldn't take her eyes off him and the little child he was helping.

"That day a school had taken the brunt of a suicide bomb and all hands were called in to help. It was a real mess. It was so sad that kids had to be dragged into grown-up chaos."

Her heart ached for the child who was sitting up on a metal bench, sticking her foot out so that Tanner could put on her shoe. She was clutching a teddy bear under one arm and stared up at him with a forlorn look on her face.

Other soldiers were in the background outfitted identically to Tanner with the same fatigues, vests and camo-covered helmets. They were going about similar duties. Still, her eyes were drawn to Tanner and the child. He looked so big standing next to the little girl. Yet, his concern was evident. It was a side of him she hadn't fathomed. Not that she doubted his compassion. He just looked so out of context in a war zone.

"What happened to the child?" she asked.

He frowned. "I don't know."

Her heart clenched and she crossed her arms protectively over her middle. Their child would grow up with every advantage. Two parents, food, shelter, safety, peace of mind. The details of how she and Tanner were coming together to make a family seemed insignificant when she considered how much worse others had it.

"Poor little girl. She must have been so frightened. Her parents must have been out of their minds with worry."

Jordana hoped he didn't see her shudder as she thought of the terror the child must've experienced, and then Jordana thought of the situation Tanner had faced; how he could've been killed like so many of the selfless men and women who'd given their lives for their country.

"You were very brave to serve over there," she whispered, a little breathless. What if he'd been in the wrong place when a bomb had exploded, or what if an enemy bullet had picked him out as easily as the photographer's camera lens had?

How different their lives might've been today. She splayed her hand over the small mound that had started to form in her middle. She drew in a deep breath and silently repeated her mantra: *everything happens for a reason.*

Tanner was alive today *for a reason.*

She dragged her gaze from the photo and looked around her new home, taking it all in. The big worries in her life had been pacifying her father and whether or not she'd die a virgin, or how she would deal with the disappointment of not realizing her dream wedding.

It all seemed a little shallow from this perspective. Sure, theirs was an out-of-wedlock pregnancy, but they would remedy that soon enough by getting married. A child—their child—was a blessing, especially at this point in her life. Seeing that photo of the little girl in the war zone and glimpsing another chapter of this complex man's life shifted everything into crystal-clear perspective.

With one last glance at the picture, she took a deep breath and made the mental leap into her new life.

Growing up, the kitchen had always been the hub of the Fortune family's busy life. Even though her mother could've hired a full-time waitstaff, she'd been way too hands-on for that. Virginia had only enlisted outside help at holidays or when her husband entertained for business purposes.

Jordana had never had to be very domestic, but as she stood in Tanner's kitchen—her kitchen—the idea intrigued her. She imagined herself in the space—cooking delicious, nutritious meals for her brood—which meant they would have more than one child…she'd always dreamed of two or three. The possibility warmed her. So did the spacious and homey room, which opened onto an even larger family room with a cavernous fireplace big enough to heat the whole house, and windows that let in a lot of light and provided an enticing glimpse into what looked like a neglected garden outside.

From the look of the bare counters and the absence of the usual chef's tools, she got the feeling Tanner didn't do much cooking. Jordana loved to cook, but thanks to her busy schedule, she didn't get a chance to indulge that pleasure very often. Plus, it never seemed to be worth the effort and mess when she was cooking only for one. It was much easier to throw together a quick salad or swing by the gourmet take-out place on the way home. Now that she was on leave from her job at Fortune South, trying a few recipes she'd collected would be a fun and rewarding way to keep herself occupied while Tanner was at work.

Getting ready for the baby would keep her plenty busy. *Speaking of—*

"Which room do you think would work best for the nursery?" she asked Tanner.

"I don't know. What do you think?"

A pensive look washed over Tanner's handsome face and for a moment, even though he was looking at Jordana, he appeared to be deep in thought.

"You know," he finally said. "Now that we're getting married, this isn't *my* house anymore. It's *our* home and I want you to feel at home here."

Maybe it was the words, but it was more the

nervous huskiness of his voice and the slightly vulnerable look in his eyes that touched her. It was sinking in—*really* sinking in—that she and Tanner were going to be a *family*.

"Thank you," she said. "That means a lot to me. I've never lived with anyone before—well, other than when I was growing up—and I wasn't quite sure how this was going to work."

He nodded and she noticed his gaze drop and linger on her mouth. Her thoughts drifted to the way his lips tasted and how they seemed to fit perfectly on hers. The memory made her bite her lower lip. They would be husband and wife soon. That meant all the perks.

To distract herself from thoughts that could drive her crazy—crazy, in the purest, best way possible—Jordana turned in a slow circle, taking in her new home. Even if the place was in need of a minor cosmetic face-lift and a woman's touch, she already had it in her heart that adding a woman's touch would be a fun and rewarding project. No, not merely a project…this wasn't work.

This was her life.

"I'm happy to give up my office to the baby, if you think that would be best."

It occurred to her that she hadn't seen the master bedroom, which, apparently, was on the other side of the house from the guest rooms and his office. That would mean that the nursery would be separated from where they slept. Sure, baby monitors were a good thing, but…

"I don't know, now that I think about it, I'd prefer for the baby to be near us at night," she said.

"Then the office will work perfectly as a nursery. You can have the master bedroom and I'll move into the spare across the hall," he said.

Spare bedroom? His words caught her off guard. "What do you mean?"

He shifted, appearing uncomfortable in the gulf of silence that spanned between them.

"What I mean is that I don't want to pressure you into anything."

Umm…?

She wanted to protest, to tell him she wanted to share a room, but she couldn't form the words. Probably because she couldn't bear the possibility of him rejecting her.

"I was thinking that for the short-term, you should have your own space. At least until you get settled in and we make everything official."

Separate bedrooms…?

His lips were moving, but she wasn't quite getting what he was telling her. Was this his way of telling her he wasn't interested in a real relationship with her? That as far as he was concerned, their marriage was little more than a business agreement?

Right now, she didn't want to know. If he was unsure, maybe he could learn to love her later. Because of that, for now, she would go along with his plan.

Her gaze meandered back to the family room and she found the photo of Tanner and the little girl.

Separate bedrooms might not be what she'd envisioned when she'd agreed to move in with Tanner. But for now, she'd count her blessings and make it work.

For now.

Chapter Eight

The next morning, Tanner was eager to show off Redmond Flight School to Jordana. And yes, if he were perfectly honest, he was eager to show her off, too.

His staff would be surprised when he told them that he, the one everyone had deemed *the confirmed bachelor,* was finally settling down. As far as he was concerned, he wanted to invite the entire staff to the wedding, but he thought he'd better confirm it with his bride-to-be before he started randomly issuing invitations.

He walked around the truck and opened her

door, offering a hand to help her down from the cab. She'd been a little quiet last night after he'd moved her luggage into her bedroom, but he'd chalked it up to exhaustion. Apparently, pregnancy was supposed to be a major drain on the mother's energy—then factor in major life changes of the engagement and the move and that was a trifecta of stress. Good stress, he hoped. But stress was stress.

She'd gone to bed early and seemed a bit more herself today. Especially after he'd suggested that she come into work with him and then take the truck and drive around a bit to reacquaint herself with the town. She seemed to like the idea. He was glad, because the sooner Red Rock started to feel like home, the happier she'd be.

The saying *A happy wife equals a happy life* came to mind. So, when she was happy, he was happy.

"Welcome to Redmond Flight School," he said as she slid off the front seat.

"Thank you." She was looking around, seemingly taking in everything.

Tanner tried to follow her gaze, wanting to see everything through her eyes. Even though the storm that brought them together had devastated the structures that housed his office and the hangar that sheltered his planes and equipment, he was suddenly very glad that everything was shiny and new.

What a paradox that tornado had been. He'd lost one of his friends and employees, Gary Tompkins, in the storm. Gary had sustained a head injury during the storm and had fallen into a coma. When the doctor removed life support, he'd eventually lost the battle. The same storm that had given Tanner his wife and child had taken his friend and colleague. It was still difficult to reconcile the two.

Tanner uttered a silent prayer of thanks to Gary. *I miss you, buddy.*

In his mind, he could see Gary's broad grin and approving thumbs-up he would've given had he met Jordana. Tanner smiled at the thought and offered his arm to his fiancée.

She took it, and as they walked, he pointed toward the small building they'd parked in front of. "That's the office—where we're going first—and the larger building in the back is the hangar. It's a pretty simple operation."

"How many employees do you have?"

"We have four. Four flight instructors and myself. And there's a guy, Max Allen, who helps out in exchange for lessons."

Thoughts of Gary loomed large in the back of

Tanner's mind, but he decided now wasn't the time to share the sad story with Jordana. He didn't want to cast a shadow on this day. Gary would've understood. So instead, Tanner paid another silent respect to his friend, unlocked the door and held it open for Jordana.

"Oh," she said when Tanner flipped on the lights.

"*Oh?* You sound disappointed."

"No, absolutely not. I just thought you'd have an office manager or receptionist."

Tanner chuckled. "I am the manager and receptionist."

"Really?" she said. "You're very hands-on."

"That's how I built my business. But actually, I've been thinking it might be time to bring on someone else to manage the office and expand our marketing endeavors. That way, I can concentrate more on flying. And with the baby on the way, it will free up some of my time."

He glanced at her, surprised at how vulnerable the huge smile on Jordana's face suddenly made him feel. He'd never been personally responsible for anyone other than himself, even though he and his siblings took pride in looking after their mom. She lived north of Tulsa, Oklahoma, nearly six hundred miles away. It was a completely different ball game when you were responsible for people under your roof, for a baby who depended on you day in and day out…for everything.

He wanted to make sure he did everything right. At least her expression seemed to indicate he'd said the right thing at the right time.

"More time for the baby…and me…is a good thing."

There was something equally vulnerable in the way she glanced up at him, looked away and then looked back, snaring his gaze. It made him feel protective and a bit alpha. She looked so fragile standing there with her guard down. He couldn't help himself. He reached out and put his arms around her, pulling her close.

She settled into him, fitting perfectly in his arms. He'd forgotten how good she felt. He buried his face in her throat, breathing in the sweet scent of her—fresh and clean, the scent of soap and shampoo, the faint hint of something floral and something uniquely her.

He kissed her throat at the tender point where the curve of her jaw gave way to the delicate slope of her neck. He felt her shudder in response. Then, as if his body was driving itself, his lips found hers in a smoldering kiss. One moment it was a leisurely and tentative lingering of lips, but then it exploded into famished need that had them parting their lips and deepening the kiss, as if their next breaths would come from each other. Tanner tried to quench his desire's thirst from her life breath. But the more he took, the more he needed. He felt her fist her hands into the collar of his shirt, leaning into him, confirming that this was indeed what she wanted. And the very thought made him pull her tighter, staking his claim, so that every inch of her was pressed up against him. Their breaths ebbed and flowed as if they'd become one, and unspoken feelings poured out in this silent affirmation of how much he wanted her.

For a moment, the whole world disappeared.

"Hello? Anybody here?"

Until a familiar voice shattered the silence and tore them from their paradise.

"Oh! Sorry, didn't mean to interrupt." It was Victoria, Jordana's cousin. The one who had outed Jordana's secret.

In a matter of seconds, Jordana's expression changed from one of rapture to that of a woman who wanted blood.

"Hi, guys!" chimed Victoria, who was all smiles. "I saw Tanner's truck outside and I thought I'd pop in and see you."

For a moment Jordana didn't say a word. She couldn't. Because she was sure if she opened her mouth she'd say a bunch of ugly things that her better judgment assured her she'd regret later. Although, right now, she was itching to tear into her big-mouthed cousin and give her a tutorial on how to mind her own business, she knew she needed to carefully weigh her words.

As the only girl and youngest child of Jordana's uncle James and aunt Clara, Victoria always did what she wanted and said what was on her mind. And she usually ended up getting what she wanted—as evidenced by the big, fat engagement ring on her left ring finger given to her by her very own real-life hero, Garrett Stone. Back in December after the tornado struck, Garrett had pulled Victoria from the rubble at the airport. Victoria had been instantly smitten.

While Jordana was happy for her cousin and hopeful that Garrett, who was fourteen years her senior, would have a maturing effect on Victoria, she was still miffed that Victoria hadn't kept her promise and had told Tanner to call Jordana before she could make up her mind how she wanted to handle the situation.

Tanner must've sensed Jordana's discomfort because he broke the silence. "Hi, Victoria. I was just giving Jordana a tour of the flight school."

Victoria's laugh sounded like two-part harmony as it mingled with the tinkle of her gold bangle bracelets that chimed when she flicked her long brown curls off her shoulder. The hair flip was one of Victoria's nervous habits, a dead giveaway that she wasn't as calm and carefree as she appeared. It made sense. Jordana hadn't spoken to her cousin since she'd spilled the beans to Tanner, giving him the news that landed him on her doorstep in Atlanta last week.

Gosh, had it been only a week? In some ways, it felt like an eternity ago. Maybe that was because even now, Jordana was having a hard time remembering her life before Tanner…and the baby.

Admitting that—and the realization that Victoria might be a tiny bit nervous—quelled Jordana's anger to a slow simmer.

Really, it was the principle of the matter that still bothered Jordana. Because obviously, the outcome had worked out. She stole a glance at Tanner. Now that she was rested, things were feeling a little more stable between them. He may not love her…yet, but at least he was willing to commit. As far as she was concerned, as long as he honored his vows and treated her and their baby well, they had the rest of their lives to fall in love.

Victoria's bangles jangled again, drawing Jordana's attention back to her. *Hmm.* Wasn't that just like Victoria?

And the fact that things were working out pretty perfectly with Tanner wasn't the point. The point was that Victoria never could keep her big mouth shut and even if Jordana was having a hard time holding on to the remnants of her initial anger, she wanted to make busybody Victoria squirm a little bit.

Finally, Jordana found her voice. "You always have had a knack for bad timing, haven't you?"

Victoria smiled and shrugged, a sheepish grin turning up the corners of her mouth. "Oh, Jor, let me see your ring." Victoria rushed forward and grabbed Jordana's hand. "Aunt Virginia told me. That's how I know you're here. *Ohmygosh,* I'm *soo* happy for you two. Jordana, we're engaged at the same time. It will be so much fun planning our weddings together."

Victoria gushed some more over Jordana's engagement ring.

"Well, I have a feeling my wedding will happen quite a bit sooner than yours because we want to get married before the baby is born. Actually, I'd like to walk down the aisle before I start showing too much more than I am now. I guess I want the focus to be on the wedding without people saying, 'Oh, look at the pregnant bride.'"

But really it wasn't an engagement in the pure meaning of the word—like Victoria and Garrett's. He'd asked her cousin to be his wife because he loved her and for no other reason. Jordana refused to kid herself about the circumstances surrounding her own engagement. Especially since she and her groom-to-be had separate bedrooms. After he'd kissed her senseless, she'd nearly forgotten about last night's awkwardness when he'd carried her bags into the master suite and relocated his things into the spare bedroom. A strange cloud of emotion momentarily shadowed the elation she'd felt seconds before, but she refused to let it drag her down.

She could focus on the positive: that he'd cared enough to track her down and refused to take no for an answer; that he'd said he didn't want to rush her—he was giving her time to get settled and acclimated to her new home before renewing their physical relationship.

She could view his taking things slowly as romantic and caring or she could conjure up negative intangibles...that maybe Tanner wasn't attracted to her. But then there was the way he'd kissed her—

"Have you already set a date?" Victoria asked breathlessly.

Jordana looked at Tanner. Their gazes snagged and lingered the way lovers might look at each other.

Ooh, he was so good at making her feel like this really could be real...

Without breaking their visual connection, he said, "Could be as early as later this week. We're going to pin down the details today."

As the butterflies rose and swooped in Jordana's stomach, Victoria squealed over the news and clapped her hands like a child who had just unlocked the secret surprise in the busy box.

In vintage Victoria fashion, she'd managed to shift the mood so that any and all residue of ill feelings that had lingered in Jordana evaporated on the spot.

Nobody could stay mad at Victoria for long. Especially when there was so much to celebrate.

"Tanner, I know you want to show her around, but if you have to work today, I'd love to take her into town and treat her to lunch," Victoria said. "We have so much catching up to do."

"Well, I do have a student coming in for a lesson in an hour or so. I was going to suggest that she take the truck and go exploring." Tanner was giving her a look that seemed to say *stop me if this is not what you want*. Jordana wondered if Victoria could read it, too. But in the next breath, Jordana realized that Victoria was probably so focused on what she wanted to do that she didn't see it. Or, even better, could Jordana dare believe that she and Tanner shared such a connection that this was something only the two of them could decipher?

Yeah, all the way across the house from his bedroom to hers.

She cleared her throat as if that would expel the negativity.

"Sure, Victoria, I'd love to have lunch."

Even though she wasn't mad at her cousin any longer, she still had a few things on her mind that Victoria needed to hear. It wouldn't hurt to make her squirm a little bit more. Next time, maybe she would think twice before she opened her mouth and blabbed prematurely.

Chapter Nine

It was the perfect day to dine alfresco, and the table in the courtyard at Red was ideal. Shaded by a cobalt umbrella that matched the shade of blue in the hand-painted Talavera tiles on the fountain's overflow pool, the pine table was situated in just the right location for people-watching and admiring the vibrant fuchsia of bougainvilleas that climbed the garden wall.

"I understand you meant well, Victoria, but that's not the point," Jordana said. "I wasn't ready to tell Tanner and you put me in such an awkward position."

Jordana was having a little too much fun nee-
dling her cousin. She shot a conspiratorial glance
at her sisters, Wendy and Emily, as they waited for
their food to be served.

When Victoria had suggested they go to lunch
at Red, the restaurant owned by Wendy's in-laws,
and managed by Wendy's husband, Marcos, Jordana knew she had better call and invite Wendy
and Emily to join them or she'd never hear the end
of it. Especially if somehow they hadn't talked to
their mother and had instead learned through the
Red Rock grapevine—or their cousin Victoria—
that Jordana was back in town.

Virginia had indeed told Wendy, who had relayed the news to Emily that their sister was moving to Red Rock…with Tanner…and with that,
Wendy had filled in the blanks and solved the
rest of the equation—that Jordana and Tanner just
might be expecting.

It was an easy conclusion, probably because
Wendy had been in a similar situation a few
months earlier. Two months after her late-
December wedding to Marcos Mendoza, the two
had celebrated the arrival of their baby daughter,
MaryAnne, who was born a month premature.

Emily had seemed a little quiet upon hearing
the news. Immediately, Jordana had regretted not

confiding in her sisters, especially when after the hugs and congratulations, Wendy had asked gently as she rocked MaryAnne to sleep, "Why didn't you tell me before now, J?"

Besides Victoria, the only other person who'd known Jordana's secret was her friend Leah Roberts. In March, as Javier Mendoza and Leah were leaving a party to welcome Wendy and Marcos's baby girl, they discovered Jordana sitting all alone on the porch looking very green in the gills. Javier tried like the dickens to convince her to go back inside so she could lie down, but Jordana refused. She was mortified that the others might find out she wasn't feeling well and put two and two together and discover she was pregnant. Her worries weren't such a far stretch because all Leah, who was a nurse, had to do was ask her a few questions and she figured out that Jordana was not "sick" but pregnant. Jordana implored her not to give away her secret. Unlike *others,* Leah was a vault.

"I hadn't even come to terms with the reality. I needed time to digest it. Time to figure out things. I wasn't even ready to tell Tanner, but Victoria helped that along."

Victoria bristled. "The way you were going, it seemed like you never were going to feel ready. So, really, I did you a favor. Your marriage to Tanner was inevitable. You belong together just like Garrett and I do."

When the food arrived, Jordana decided to call off the dogs. Victoria had her convictions and seemed to truly believe that because it worked out for Garrett and her that it would work out for Jordana and Tanner.

As feelings of hope blossomed in Jordana's heart, she realized she wanted to believe her in the worst way.

Maybe she should borrow a page from Victoria's book of optimism, which at times Jordana had thought of as immature and idealistic, and change her mind-set.

As the Fortune women raised their glasses and toasted each other with sparkling water, Jordana silently toasted her new life with Tanner in Red Rock and all the possibilities that lay ahead.

"So," Victoria said to Wendy and Emily. "This morning, Tanner said that the wedding might happen as soon as this weekend. We have a lot of planning to do."

Wendy gently shifted MaryAnne from her right arm to her left so she could eat her salad while the baby slept. Jordana looked on in wonder at how naturally maternal Wendy seemed. It was as if she'd been born to have a baby in her arms. "Have you made any plans at all yet?"

"No. I don't even know where to begin since I don't really know the town. This has all happened so fast that I haven't had a chance to check out our options here in Red Rock."

"Well, that's where we can help," said Victoria. "So, I guess the best place to start with is where you want to have the ceremony. Inside or outside?"

Jordana's plan for her ideal wedding had been quite traditional. The ceremony would've taken place in the church she'd attended since she was a child. She wanted a bridal party that went on for days and a dress with a train that stretched into next week. There'd been plans for at least three flower girls and a ring bearer.

But here in Red Rock there was no church from childhood; the only child she knew was her infant niece, who was obviously much too young to toss flower petals; and she'd be lucky if her sisters and cousin would agree to stand up with her. In fact, she didn't even know if her parents were going to be amenable to flying in, given her refusal of the quickie wedding they had offered.

"Outside, I guess? I don't know. Is there a nice garden close by?"

Wendy, Emily and Victoria all started talking

at once, throwing out ideas for possible venues, flowers and dress shopping. By the time lunch was over they'd made a list of places to visit that afternoon.

Jordana had forgotten how much she enjoyed her family outside of the business arena. So much of her life had been centered around her job at Fortune South she hadn't realized what it was like to let down her hair and enjoy herself without considering trends and market share and such.

For a moment, she wondered if she should give Tanner an update, tell him that the Fortune women had taken their wedding and were running with it.

Then as if tuned into that invisible connection that tied the two of them together, her cell phone rang. Tanner's name flashed on the screen.

"Hi, Tanner."

The girls hushed and turned their attention to Jordana when they heard her say his name.

"Hi. Are you having a good day?"

"I am. We're just finishing up lunch at Red. Have you had lunch yet? Do you want me to bring you something?"

"Thanks, but I've already eaten. Glad you're having fun. Red is a great place. It's one of my favorites."

"Yes, it is. I'd heard Wendy say so many good things about it, I was dying to try it."

"We'll have to go back for dinner sometime. But in the meantime, I made some calls about the marriage license. There's a three-day waiting period. But other than that, we're good to go. How soon do you want to go down to the courthouse and apply? If we do it today or tomorrow, we can get married Thursday or Friday."

Hearing the words nearly knocked the breath out of her. This was really real. She was going to marry Tanner Redmond.

"I'm up for either day, seeing how my schedule is pretty open. What works best for you?"

"I don't want to interrupt your afternoon with Victoria and your sisters…"

"No, you're not. Would today work?"

"Yes, I was thinking the sooner we got through all the official red tape the sooner we could start our life together."

His words unleashed the butterflies again. Did that mean he was as eager as she was to do this? Since everything seemed to be pointing that way, she was going to let herself believe it was true.

"How about if I have Victoria drop me back by the office once we're finished here."

"Or actually, you know what I could do? Why

don't you all go downtown and I'll meet you there. That way you won't have to backtrack."

It was a plan.

Once they hung up, Jordana relayed the news to the girls. "We're getting our marriage license today. We're getting married Thursday or Friday."

Five days later, Tanner found himself pacing in front of the fountain at the Red Rock Botanical Gardens on his and Jordana's wedding day. Even though he wasn't allowing himself to have second thoughts—that wasn't an option—he couldn't deny he was more nervous today than he'd been on his first solo flight.

The guests were just beginning to arrive for the seven o'clock ceremony. To steady his nerves as he waited, he went out to the site where he would take his vows to take in every detail of the elegant scene: the bushels of flowers—both imported for the ceremony and growing naturally in the garden—they were adorned with tiny white twinkle lights; the snow-white runner that stretched from the trellis at the back of the ceremony space to the front by the fountain where he and Jordana would exchange their vows; and the candles encased in glass lamps that lined the fountain and added an extra romantic touch. All the trimmings and little luxuries—including a courtyard dinner at Red after the ceremony—that Jordana and her family had somehow managed to pull together over the span of seventy-two hours to make this an evening he and Jordana would remember forever.

The scene both warmed and terrified him. And if he was feeling this way, he wondered where Jordana's head was right about now. She'd been the one with the most trepidation. Her parents, who had flown in yesterday for the ceremony, had tried to warn him that she might run. Now he wondered if he should've listened to them and gone along with the ceremony they'd tried to rope her into back in Atlanta.

No. He had to trust that he'd done the right thing waiting to get married here. It was right because it was what Jordana wanted. He had to trust her, because if they were going to build a life together, they would have nothing without a foundation of trust. Not everyone ran out on their families like his father had done.

He had to trust that Jordana would keep her promise.

He pushed the thoughts out of his mind, telling himself that the only reason he was feeling this way was because he hadn't seen Jordana since last night when their families had met for the rehearsal dinner, which had been catered by the Mendozas, but served at his and Jordana's house.

Even though the wedding was shaping up to be more unconventional than Jordana had wanted, she had still insisted on sticking to some of the timeless traditions—such as the bride and groom not seeing each other on their wedding day until the ceremony.

He took a deep breath and raked his hands through his close-cropped hair.

Everything would be fine once he saw his bride walking down the aisle. It was ten minutes until seven. It wouldn't be long.

The groomsmen were busy serving as ushers, seating people as they arrived. His brother, Parker, waved at him as he finished showing Leah Roberts and Javier Mendoza to their seats.

"You hanging in there, bro?" he asked, giving Tanner a playful sock on the biceps.

"I'm doing great. Are the women here yet?"

"Not as far as I know. But then again, they could be secreted off somewhere I don't know about."

"Did you happen to see a big black limousine out front?"

"Nope. Nothing like that."

Tanner's gut gave an uncomfortable twist. Jordana had spent the night at her sister Wendy's house last night after the rehearsal. That's where they were getting ready today. A limo would be bringing her and the bridal party to the gardens.

He glanced at his watch again.

One minute later than when he'd checked the first time. Everything would be fine, he reassured himself. There was still plenty of time and there was no reason for Jordana to stand around while people were being seated. In fact, since the plan was for her to go straight from the limo to walking down the aisle, she'd probably wait to arrive until seven.

It would be the longest nine minutes of Tanner's life.

To distract himself he greeted people, shaking hands and exchanging hugs and slaps on the back with friends and colleagues. He reminded himself how grateful he was that his entire family—his mother, sister and brother—were able to be here today. That was one of the reasons he and Jordana had decided to wait the extra couple of days to hold the ceremony on Saturday—so that it would be more convenient for extended family to fly in.

Parker had agreed to stand up with him and be his best man. Tanner's flight instructors Jonathan,

Ross, Brody, Paul and Simon had agreed to serve as ushers and groomsmen.

They would be paired with Jordana's attendants: co-maids of honor Wendy and Emily; and bridesmaids Victoria; Tanner's younger sister, Laurel; Christina Hastings and Katie Wallace. The latter two were the fiancées of her brothers, Scott and Blake.

According to Jordana, it was unheard of for the attendants to nearly outnumber the guests, but since nothing about this union was *conventional* she was throwing tradition to the wind. Thank God it seemed to be blowing back blessings and good fortunes, because it was a picture-perfect evening and everything seemed to be proceeding without a hitch.

There had been only one slight hiccup in the plans. He and Jordana would have to delay their honeymoon. The FAA was due to come out and perform an inspection now that the flight school was fully operational after the storm. The problem was that the inspections were never scheduled. They were always done on a surprise basis. Even though it would be highly in Tanner's favor to be there during the inspection, he had been willing to chance it and go away for a few nights. However, Jordana had insisted that they wait to go away until after the inspection was signed and sealed. That way, she said, Tanner would be able to relax and enjoy himself.

In addition, Jordana had told him it was important to her to get settled in as soon as possible. The rest of her belongings were being shipped from Atlanta and were due to arrive next week. The pregnancy and the morning sickness had zapped her energy, so she wanted to give herself plenty of time to put everything away and get the baby's nursery in order. Once those tasks were accomplished, she said she, too, would be able to enjoy herself more. She'd assured him that if they could take time together to explore Red Rock—if he would show her some of his favorite places—that would be a perfect honeymoon. At least for now.

Suddenly, the string quintet and harpist struck up Pachelbel's Canon in D. His mother appeared under the archway of the flower-covered trellis on the arm of Jordana's youngest brother, Blake, who was escorting her to her seat.

The minister took his place near the fountain and an awed hush of anticipation fell over the small group that had gathered to witness the exchange of vows and union of souls. Tanner rubbed his clammy hands on his trousers and then reached into his pocket to pull out the index card with his vows written on it. He moved into place, and smiled at his mother, whose eyes were glistening with tears, but the huge smile on her face assured him that they were indeed happy tears.

Next, Virginia was escorted down the aisle on the arms of her two sons, Blake and Scott.

Finally, the quintet reached the end of the Pachelbel. Tanner drew in a nervous deep breath, awaiting them to strike up the first strains of the "Wedding March" and to see Jordana's bridesmaids appear one by one in the archway.

Time seemed to stand still and freeze. Tanner waited, yet still no music and no bridesmaids. Finally, the guests seemed to grow restless as whispered questions about *What's going on? Where's the bride? I hope everything's okay* hung in the air.

Tanner glanced at Virginia, whose mouth was drawn into a grim line. She gave a very slight shake of her head and a shrug, indicating she didn't understand what was going on, either.

In the span of a heartbeat, Tanner worried that his worst nightmare might be playing out right in front of all his friends and colleagues.

Had Jordana changed her mind?

Chapter Ten

"Victoria, it's one thing to be late to your own wedding, but to make the bride late to her wedding... Aren't bridesmaids supposed to help, not hinder?" Tanner ribbed his new cousin-in-law as the entire family gathered for Mother's Day brunch the day after the wedding.

Jordana watched Victoria's cheeks flush a pretty shade of pink. She wasn't sure if it was from embarrassment or irritation.

"I said I was sorry," Victoria said. "I told you I had to take care of some—" she cleared her throat "—*personal business* once we got to the gardens.

I had to pee, okay? And then I took a wrong turn down a path that led me to the other side of the property. Are you happy now? Do you have any idea how hard it is to trudge around in the grass in four-inch heels?"

The more Victoria talked the harder everyone laughed. Knowing her cousin, she was loving every second of the attention.

"If *someone* would've waited for me rather than getting impatient—" she shot a rather pointed look at Wendy "—it never would've happened. So, you see, really it's not even my fault."

As everyone laughed, Jordana continued to fake a smile and a chuckle. She wasn't in a very festive mood this morning, but since her mother and Tanner's mom, Shirley, were here on Mother's Day, she was forcing herself to play the part of the blushing bride on the morning after her wedding.

Why not? She was getting very good at pretending to be something she wasn't. Today's masquerade involved sitting next to Tanner and pretending to be very much in love—which wasn't such a stretch. What was difficult was keeping herself from crying when she thought of how she hadn't shared a traditional wedding night with her husband of less than twenty-four hours. When in reality, they'd slept in separate rooms...again.

"I am so happy that my son has *finally* decided to settle down," Shirley cooed. "And Jordana, sweetheart, I couldn't have handpicked anyone better for him."

She'd loved Shirley at first sight. Jordana was indeed blessed in the mother-in-law department. But the marriage bed was another story.

In fact, the words *what marriage bed* more aptly described their situation.

At first, she'd thought his not wanting to pressure her, his wanting her to get *settled in* was sweet and considerate, but now it was getting downright frustrating. And she didn't know how to tell him.

His arm was draped casually across the back of her chair. If she leaned back she could feel the weight of his arm and the heat of his skin on her shoulders. Anybody looking at them would believe they were very much in love.

She wanted that so desperately, because somewhere between being angry at him when he showed up unannounced on her doorstep and sitting here feeling alone in this crowd of family, she'd realized she lost her heart to him along the way. It was the most helpless, hopeless feeling... especially because she had no idea if he felt the same way.

On one hand, she couldn't ask for him to treat her with any more respect, but on the other, his lack of physical interest made him appear a little standoffish.

They hadn't written their own vows, but still, reciting the ones the minister had provided meant just as much. She could still see the earnest expression on his handsome face and hear his voice as he said, "I, Tanner, take you, Jordana, to be my wife, my partner in life and my one true love. I will cherish our union and love you more each day than I did the day before. I will trust you and respect you, laugh with you and cry with you, loving you faithfully through good times and bad, regardless of the obstacles we may face together. I give you my hand, my heart and my love, from this day forward for as long as we both shall live."

Love.

Four times in the span of a marriage-vow recitation, he'd promised to love her. Yet, last night, he couldn't seem to get away from her fast enough.

Well, right now, there was nothing she could do about it. She took a deep breath and promised herself she would do her best to focus on the family that had come such a long way to celebrate their wedding…and the subsequent news that they were expecting a baby toward the end of September.

Across the table, Wendy was trying to jockey a squirmy MaryAnne and eat her Eggs Benedict. Since she really needed two hands to cut through the Canadian bacon and English muffin, she was having a hard time, and MaryAnne seemed to sense her mother's frustration and was beginning to fuss.

Since Jordana was finished with her brunch, she asked, "Wendy, may I hold my niece, please?"

"Seriously?" Wendy asked, as if the offer of help was a novel idea never before presented as a choice.

"Absolutely," Jordana proclaimed. She stood up and walked around the table and took the sweet-smelling little bundle into her arms. Tanner was deep in conversation with his brother and didn't seem to notice. So she decided to take little Mary-Anne out to the neglected garden for a bit of fresh air.

It was a beautiful day with temperatures hovering in the low-to-mid-seventies. Jordana breathed in the fresh scent of spring in full swing. That, mixed with the scent of baby, was just about as close to the smell of heaven one could experience on earth.

There wasn't a cloud in the robin's-egg-blue sky and Jordana thought for a minute that she could quite easily spend the rest of the afternoon out here. Of course, it would be nicer if the garden was planted and tended, but it didn't really bother her since reviving the courtyard would be a welcome treat in the weeks to come...after she got the baby's nursery set up, of course.

Maybe if she stayed out here no one would see the sadness in her eyes. She walked over and settled herself on a stone bench.

MaryAnne kicked her little legs and cooed up at her, and Jordana couldn't help but smile back. Leave it to a baby to draw out the best in an adult, whether the adult wanted to be drawn out or not. Her niece was a beautiful baby, who seemed to have equal parts of Wendy and Marcos in her.

Jordana found herself wondering what hers and Tanner's baby would look like... Would she have Tanner's dark hair or her fair tresses? Would he be tall and lanky like her father or built more like her? Heaven help him if he was.

For that matter, would they be blessed with a girl or a boy?

As Jordana gently rocked sweet MaryAnne back and forth, mesmerized by the baby and all her small, perfect parts, she decided on the spot that either one would be fine as long as their child was healthy. And no, she didn't want to know the baby's sex before the birth because that felt too much like opening a Christmas present before December twenty-fifth.

The sound of a door opening and footsteps made her look up. Her sister Emily was poised in the doorway, watching Jordana. A peculiar sort of Mona Lisa smile teased the edges of her lips. Jordana couldn't tell if she looked melancholy or content.

"You're a natural," Emily said, as she walked into the courtyard and took a seat next to Jordana on the bench.

"It's easy with one as sweet as this," Jordana said. "I mean, who would've ever thought that out of the three of us, Wendy would be a mother first?"

"I know. To be honest, I guess I'm a little jealous. I never thought you would be second. Or should I say, I never thought I'd be the last of us."

As a warm breeze blew and rustled the tree branches, Emily offered her pinky to MaryAnne. The baby latched on, her tiny fingers curving around Emily's as if her life depended on it. In turn, Emily was gazing down at the baby as if her own life hung in the balance.

Emily was jealous?

"Believe me," Jordana said, searching for words

to make her sister feel better. "When I heard the news that I was pregnant, I was just as flabbergasted as you are. Having a baby right now was not on my list of New Year's resolutions."

Emily laughed, but there was no humor in the sound. "And that's the cruel irony. It's at the very top of my list."

Despite the note of desperation in her voice, Jordana did a double take to see if her sister was being facetious.

"Really?" she asked.

"You know me, Jordana. All my life, I have wanted nothing more than to be a mother."

She did know her sister—or at least she thought she did—but she didn't realize how badly Emily wanted to have a baby. Emily wasn't like Victoria, who had a streak of wanting what she didn't have. Emily was solid. She didn't take things lightly or do things halfway thought out. That's how she'd been at school and in the office at Fortune South. Perhaps that's why this declaration of hers was so surprising. Since Emily didn't have any solid romantic prospects, having a baby didn't seem to fit into her life right now. Obviously, Jordana had it all wrong.

Emily shrugged, as if trying to convince herself. "I figured why wait around for love to dictate my future when I can take matters into my own capable hands?"

Now, *that* was so like her practical, get-the-job-done sister. If she saw a practical solution, even if it wasn't conventional, she went for it. She'd always been that way as far back as Jordana could remember.

"The only problem is I haven't had much luck making any progress. At first, I thought I'd adopt, but so far, I have not been able to locate any potential birth mothers willing to give their baby to a single woman. I guess I can understand that—they want their child to grow up in a traditional home. But you know me. I won't let a small setback like that get in my way."

"What are you going to do?" Slowly, Jordana adjusted her hold on MaryAnne, who was beginning to drift off to sleep.

"I have an appointment with a fertility doctor in Atlanta."

"Get out," Jordana whispered, not wanting to wake the baby. "Are you serious?"

"I've never been more serious in my life. I already have a sperm donor lined up. I could be pregnant in a matter of weeks."

Jordana gaped at her sister. Emily was going to such great lengths to conceive, and all it took Jordana was one night of unprotected sex, and bam, she was in the family way. If she hadn't already bonded with her unborn baby and decided that, despite the circumstances, this was absolutely what she wanted, she might feel a little guilty. But all the guilt in the world wouldn't give Emily a child. So what was the point? Especially when despite the picture-perfect veneer, her own situation was less than ideal. The best thing she could do for her unborn child was to love it unconditionally.

"Just think how wonderful it will be if you and I are pregnant at the same time. Our kids will all be around the same age and will grow up together."

Jordana laughed. "MaryAnne, you can be the bossy one since you'll be the oldest. That's the job of the oldest of the Fortune girls."

"Hey!" Emily protested, smiling and looking much more like herself now that she'd shared her secret. "That's the oldest Fortune girl's prerogative."

"Does Mama know?" Jordana asked.

"Heck, no." Emily's eyes were as wide as the saucer-sized magnolia blossoms on the trees lining the courtyard. "And I'd appreciate it if you didn't say anything to her just yet. I know she's been understanding and supportive with you and Wendy, but if the truth be told, she didn't have much choice. In my case, however, it's completely different and she will be on me like white on rice trying to change my mind about having a baby on my own." Emily put up her hands as if to ward off their mother's meddling. "She's not going to change my mind, but I don't even want to have to go there before everything is set in stone."

Jordana blew out a breath. "Your secret's safe with me, but whatever you do, don't breathe a word to Victoria."

"What secret?" Tanner's voice made both Jordana and Emily jump. They hadn't heard him open the door and come outside. The sight of him made Jordana's heart do a little hiccup.

"Just girl talk," Jordana said.

There was no denying the man—her husband, for God's sake—was off-the-charts gorgeous.

The thrill lasted only a nanosecond before she reminded herself how her gorgeous husband had removed himself from her bed. Even on their wedding night. The dark cloud that had shadowed her all morning returned.

I didn't get married to live like a nun, Tanner Redmond. You and I are going to have a serious talk after everyone leaves, and if it takes tying you to the bedposts, I'm going to—

"Oh, okay. Well, I hate to do this, but I have to

go to work for a little while. There's some business I need to take care of."

"On Mother's Day?" She didn't mean to sound so incredulous, but she couldn't mask her disappointment. It just slipped out.

"Yes, I'm sorry. I know it's Mother's Day, but just so you're aware, the nature of my job sometimes requires me to work on Sundays. Sometimes that's the only day my students are available for lessons."

"And you didn't know this before now? I mean, we have a house full of company, many who have come a long way to help us celebrate our wedding—"

Sham! Sham! Sham! The word blared in her head like a siren.

"I meant to tell you earlier, but with all the excitement over the wedding, it slipped my mind. I'm really sorry, Jordana. Please try to understand."

Oh, she understood all right. She was the queen of demanding jobs. After all, she'd practically been married to hers before Tanner came in and plucked her out of it. And now he was expecting her to be at his beck and call and understand when he decided to waltz out at a moment's notice.

Through the fog of her irritation, she became

aware of Emily glancing back and forth between the two of them. She didn't want to get into it any deeper in front of her sister. Ha! And risk exposing the truth that this marriage wasn't as perfect as everyone might believe?

"What about your mother and brother and sister?"

"Parker is going to hang out with your brothers and watch a little baseball on television. I thought maybe you girls could go downtown for a while."

"Hey, why don't we go down to the Stocking Stitch and visit Maria? When we were out to lunch at Red, you were saying you wanted to learn to knit. Now would be the perfect time to go. I'm sure Maria would love it if we all descended upon her."

Jordana had met Maria Mendoza for the first time last night at the wedding. A fixture in Red Rock, Maria's knitting shop was the hub of friendship and gossip in Red Rock. Actually, the longer the idea sank in, the better it sounded.

"It's Mother's Day, surely Maria's not working today."

"Of course she's working. She's always at the Stocking Stitch."

Jordana took a deep breath. It really was a good idea, as much as she hated to admit it, she cursed her pregnancy hormones and the wild ride they'd been taking her on since day one. *Gaaah,* she desperately wanted to get a handle on them. Maybe knitting would be a therapeutic means of doing just that. Not to mention a good place to take the ladies so they could escape *sports central,* which the guys were getting ready to create.

"How does that sound?" Tanner asked. His voice had lost the challenging edge it had carried before. As Jordana nodded her concession, she even thought she saw a hint of…what…? There was something in his eyes.

Something.

It was that same *something* that kept reeling her back to him and driving her crazy with want, when common sense told her to run like the wind from this less-than-perfect situation.

"Good," Tanner said, and pulled her into a hug. "Don't worry, I won't be gone long. Okay?"

Well, she didn't exactly have a choice, did she? No, she didn't. So, this afternoon, she would occupy herself and their guests at the Stocking Stitch and keep up the front. But tonight, when she and Tanner were alone, she intended to lay some new ground rules for their marriage.

Chapter Eleven

Tanner hated arguing with Jordana. But the woman had a stubborn streak that wouldn't bend. Actually, that wasn't completely true. She'd conceded this afternoon, hadn't she?

A wave of regret washed over him as he steered the Tahoe into the garage at home. He was the one who had been in the wrong this time. After thinking about it for a while, he could see that clearly. He should've told her he had an appointment before he was walking out the door. In fact, he should've just rescheduled it.

But when he'd scheduled it, he had no idea it

would be the day after his wedding and that he'd
have a house full of company celebrating Mother's
Day. Because of his trip to Atlanta, the wedding
plans and the day-to-day business of Redmond
Flight School, he and Max Allen had been having
a dickens of a time aligning their schedules so they
could discuss the possibility of Max coming on as
an official member of the Redmond team. If they
hadn't met today, it would have been another ten
days before they could have carved out a mutually
convenient time to sit down and talk business.

He hadn't had time to explain it to Jordana,
but she was one of the key reasons it was so important that he talked to Max sooner rather than
later. He was sure once he gave her the details, she
would see the beauty in why he had to leave: this
afternoon, he had offered Max Allen a job, which
would ease some of the load off Tanner.

It was only a part-time and provisional marketing and office manager position to start off. But
based on the way Max had already proven himself as he'd worked around the school to earn his
flying lessons while he worked full-time over at
the Double Crown Ranch, Tanner had a gut feeling Max would soon make it worthwhile to bring
him on full-time.

He couldn't wait to share the good news with

his wife. On the way home, he'd even stopped at the garden shop and picked up a present for her: a pink rosebush. She'd been talking about how eager she was to get her hands in the dirt out in the garden, and Tanner figured it would be her first plant.

He'd felt so bad about the way he'd messed up today—he hadn't even gotten the mother of his unborn child a Mother's Day present. That realization had reached out and slapped him in the face not long after he'd left the house for his appointment with Max. So, when he'd stopped by the florist on the way home, he'd picked up a dozen roses. He'd had a brainstorm: since he was guilty of two relationship *crimes* he wanted to bring her two *I'm sorry* presents—a dozen red roses and a rosebush that would last forever.

Since it was nearly seven o'clock and dinner-time, he'd also stopped and picked up some Chinese takeout and a bottle of her favorite papaya juice for dinner. All the cars were gone, and he was hoping they would finally have some time alone. He'd made arrangements to spend time with his mother and siblings tomorrow before they left, but right now his soul needed some peace and quiet and some uninterrupted time with his *wife*.

Armed with the bouquet of roses in one hand

and the container with the rosebush tucked under his other arm, he opened the door to a quiet house. There was a light on in the hallway, but the rest of the place was dark.

"Jordana, hello? I'm home."

There was no answer.

He set the rosebush in the hall and went back outside to the sack of Chinese and juice. As he stepped back into the quiet house, for a fleeting moment, a flash of fear shot through him. That maybe she'd been so angry with him that she'd decided to exercise that damn *escape clause* she'd insisted on before she'd agreed to marry him. But then as he made his way toward the kitchen to unload the dinner, he heard strains of classical music coming from the vicinity of the master bedroom.

Ahhh, maybe she hadn't heard him when he'd called her name. Or, maybe she had and was still mad at him. Clutching the bouquet of roses, he headed toward the back part of the house.

"Jordana?"

"I'm in here," she called. "Come in."

He pushed open the door and hesitantly entered. The bedroom and bath had been remodeled into one with an open floor plan, and as he stood in the center of the room turning in a slow circle, he caught sight of her in the bathtub.

"Oh, I'm sorry," he said, turning away. "I'll give you some privacy."

As he turned to leave, she called him back. "Tanner, wait."

He stopped in his tracks, clutching the bouquet, but kept his back turned to her.

"I didn't mean to interrupt. I can come back after you're finished."

He heard the sound of splashing, as if she were getting out of the tub. Then she appeared in front of him wearing a silky robe that clung to her gorgeous body, beads of water dripping from the exposed skin that the robe didn't cover.

Arousal hot and urgent shot through him and he had to suck in a deep breath to keep from reaching out and pulling her into his arms.

"What's wrong with you? *Err,* what's wrong with *us?* Or *me?*" Her voice shook so badly he thought she was going to burst into tears.

"Tanner, do you find me so unattractive that you can't even look at me, much less sleep with me like a husband sleeps with his wife?"

He blinked. It took a moment for the meaning of what she was saying to fully sink in.

She thought he didn't want her?

Oh, hell no.

Tanner was so good to her in every way. She couldn't understand why he was holding back in this area of their relationship. Unless it was that he simply didn't find her attractive.

The possibility crushed her. She'd come so far trusting him—and he'd lived up to all that he'd promised.

Except in the bedroom. And that promise had been unspoken, given the night they'd made love.

Even so, she intended to hold him to it because she desperately wanted more of what he'd given her that first night. The only problem was that somewhere along the way he'd changed his mind.

As Jordana watched him stand there frozen, his eyes locked to hers as if he couldn't bear to look down, she thought this just might be one of the most humiliating moments of her life.

The man to whom she'd given her virginity found her so repulsive he couldn't even speak. Was it because she'd gotten so fat? She was almost five months along, she'd just popped and—okay, she'd admit it, she was feeling sort of insecure. When a man refused to sleep with a woman it tended to have that effect. Or at least it did on her.

Had her lovemaking been *that* bad? Sure, she was inexperienced, but despite it being her first time, it had been good for her. She'd wanted him again. Judging from his reaction, she'd believed it had been good for him, too.

Obviously she was sadly mistaken.

It would be the hardest thing she'd ever done, but tomorrow she would pack her bags and fly back to Atlanta with her parents. She could handle divorce proceedings from there.

"Just leave," she whispered, barely able to say the words.

As she turned to walk away, she felt Tanner's hand on her shoulder.

"Is that what you think? That I'm not attracted to you? I would laugh if that weren't so far from the truth."

"No, I believe my exact words were that you are *repulsed* by me. Does that better describe the situation?"

He opened his mouth to say something, but no words came out until he gave his head a quick shake that dislodged the block.

"That is most ridiculous thing I've ever heard. You are the most desirable, attractive, drive-a-man-out-of-his-damn-mind-with-want woman I have ever met. It has been killing me to have you so close and not *have* you. But sex was not part of our arrangement, and I wasn't about to force you into anything."

"Arrangement? Is that all this is to you? A business deal?"

She didn't understand what kind of game he was playing. So, she tried to pull out of his grasp, but he wouldn't let her.

"Jordana, you have no idea how difficult it's been to keep my hands off you. But I promised you from the beginning I would never force you into anything."

What? Why—

"*Why* would you want to keep your hands off me unless you couldn't stand to touch me? This sounds like one great big sorry excuse."

He blew out a breath that sounded sort of like he'd been holding the weight of the world on his shoulders and sort of like her question…amused him?

Again, she tried to pull away, but he wouldn't let her go. "I have been keeping my hands off you because of the intense passion we shared that one night we were together. I've been so afraid if I made love to you we'd risk hurting the baby."

Now it was her turn to shake her head and look at him dumbfounded. "What? That's crazy."

He frowned. "No, it's not. It's using common sense. That's one of the main reasons I suggested we have separate rooms, because I knew if I even tried to sleep next to you, I wouldn't be able to keep my hands off you. That's how much I want you."

As the sincerity of his words sank in, she couldn't deny that it felt good to have someone so protective of her and the baby.

"The doctor assured me that there was no harm in gentle lovemaking. In fact, he said it would be a really good idea if it helped relax me. Believe me, right about now, it would be a *really* good idea."

They both stood there transfixed. He looked unsure of what to do. So, she said, "You said you'd never force me into anything I wasn't ready for, right?"

He nodded.

"Well, please, please don't force me into a marriage without a physical relationship."

She squeezed her eyes closed for a moment because what she was thinking was difficult to put into words. Then it all came out in one rushing gush. "We are not doing anything wrong. We *are* married, after all, and the doctor told me that it is fine for the baby if we have sex. What I need more than anything right now is to be in my husband's arms—in your bed. Tanner, I want you."

He'd laughed, but somehow the mirth in his voice didn't make it all the way to his eyes. There was that look again. That gaze of his that reached all the way down into her soul and plucked the heartstrings at the very core of her. And the next thing she knew he'd pulled her into his arms and was holding her. He'd been holding a bouquet of roses a moment ago, but they were on the ground now.

She didn't care as long as she was in his arms. That was all that mattered.

His mouth found hers and came down on it hard and fast.

She was so full of want and need for him, feeling him respond to her was the most powerful aphrodisiac she could imagine existed. She caressed the outline of his shoulders, tracing the sinewy cords of muscle down his arms. She let her hands linger on his biceps, savoring the feel of his firm muscles. Then she slid her hands back and over the expanse of his back, working her way down until her fingers stopped at the vee of his waist. She reveled in the feel of how his broad back narrowed at the waist, at the sheer masculine width and breadth of him.

The movement pressed the most intimate parts of their bodies together, and even though he stood there unmoving, she could feel his desire pressing into her.

Even if he was standing perfectly still, she knew as she gazed up at him, searching his face, his eyes, his lips, that he wanted her, too.

He slid his hands up her arms, until he found the collar of her robe and pushed the silky fabric until it slid off her shoulders and down her arms. Pulling her tighter against him, fully enfolding her into his body. "Please tell me you're not still worried?"

Rather than answering, he showed her. He ravished her mouth, bold and hungry—there was nothing tentative between them like there had been since their wedding. The way he was kissing and touching her made it feel like the first time, when they hadn't been able to keep their hands off each other. It was as if every brush of lips and tongue, every tender caress and sweep of fingertips had been saved up for this moment.

Without taking his mouth off hers, he backed her across the bedroom, and as she felt the edge of the bed at the bend of her knees, Tanner eased her down onto the mattress.

He tugged at the belt of the robe and then

pushed it away so that she lay naked in the moon-light. When he took a nipple into his mouth, need coursed through her, hot and greedy.

It had been so long, she was surprised she didn't melt under the heat of his hands. It was the feel of those hands on her body, the touch of his rugged fingers on her sensitive skin that kept her focused, though just barely, and made her arch under him, claiming exactly what she wanted. The world seemed to fade away as Tanner explored her body with his mouth and hands. He kissed and teased and tormented her, taking her to the brink of places she hadn't visited since their first time together.

She tugged his shirt over his head, then slid her hands between them and worked his zipper, then with his help, she tugged away his pants until they lay there, skin on skin, and there was nothing be-tween them except pure desire.

He parted her legs and she was hungry for the feel of him. She needed every masculine inch of him on top of her, the sexy weight of him bear-ing down on her. The mere feel of him made her body shudder. The only thing that could be better was if he was inside her. As if reading her mind, he nestled himself into the space between her legs and gently moved his hips forward.

"Are you all right?" he asked.

She nodded.

"I want to take it slowly. And you have to tell me if something doesn't feel right. I don't want to hurt you or the baby."

With a single stroke he entered her.

Jordana gasped from the sheer pleasure of him inside her.

His breathing rasped against her temple. He pulled out then thrust a little deeper.

"Are you okay?" he asked.

"I've never felt better," she whispered, barely able to whisper the words.

She clung to him, matching him thrust for thrust, ebbing and flowing over and over until waves of pleasure crashed around her.

Finally, it could've been minutes or hours later, Tanner's breath was ragged and hot against her cheek and he gently increased the speed of his thrusts until he gave a final plunge and a long, satisfied groan erupted in his throat. He collapsed next to her, turning her body to face him so he could kiss her tenderly, possessively, as they reveled in their spent pleasure.

Chapter Twelve

Tanner pulled back a little so that he could revel in the beauty of her face as his lips still brushed hers.

"Are you sure you're okay?" he asked.

"Yes. I'm fine. I'm better than fine. The baby and I will not break, okay?"

He loved the fact that she had a mind of her own and that she wasn't afraid to speak it. He'd always heard that the key to any good relationship was communication. If that was the case, they would be just fine.

"So, when is your next doctor's appointment?"

He pulled her tighter against him. "I want to go with you."

"I'd love for you to come with me. Then you can hear with your own ears that lovemaking will not hurt the baby. In fact, it will be good for him or her."

"Good for him? How so?"

"Are you familiar with the saying *A happy wife makes a happy life?*"

He laughed. "Very funny."

"Actually, since I have to carry the child, lovemaking can be your contribution to the pregnancy."

"Oh, I see where this is going. You'll carry the baby and I will be your personal sex slave?"

The mere thought had him primed and ready to go again, but even though she'd assured him that *gentle lovemaking* was fine, he wasn't sure about how often was healthy for the child. Jordana could be pretty assertive—that was what had turned him on that night of the storm; memories of that night had kept him going as he pursued her.

And now she was in his bed where she belonged…

Still holding her, he angled his hips to give himself space to come back down to earth. She snuggled in closer to him, breathing a contented sigh.

"Let's never wait that long again," she said, her breath hot on his neck.

"I'm with you on that," he said. "If I mess up again, you have to tell me."

"What do you mean?"

"Sometimes I can be a little dense. You know, sometimes I'm not very good at reading the handwriting on the wall. Especially if the writing is subtle."

"So, you're saying I need to spell things out in large, bold strokes?"

"Exactly. Like our first night together…the night the tornado hit and we ended up in the hunting lodge. You let me know in *large, bold strokes* exactly what you wanted. Very sexy, by the way. I've been dying to tell you that." He planted a slow, lingering kiss on her lips to drive home the point. The way she responded to him did not help his resolution to limit the lovemaking until he could talk to the doctor about frequency and intensity.

So, he pulled away and resorted to talking to regain control of himself.

"All right, so you've told me how you were feeling—and I do hope I've proven to you that I am a good listener, that I understand everything you were saying."

She laughed and the sound of her voice infused

him with a longing that couldn't be quenched by making love all day, every day. It sort of took him by surprise, stole his breath for a minute, in the same way a well-placed kick in the gut will leave you breathless.

The feeling was foreign and a little bit uncomfortable, but he tried to ignore it.

"As I was saying, I have a question for you."

"Okay," she said. "Fire away."

"That first night—the one with the big, bold strokes—how come you haven't been that… umm…well, for lack of better words…how come you haven't been that sexually assertive since we've been back together? I like that side of you."

The hand that had been stroking his chest stilled. He felt her tense, pull away ever so slightly.

"Well, I guess if this is the night of full disclosure, there's something I need to tell you."

She shifted and lifted herself up on one elbow so that they were looking at each other, face-to-face.

"That sexually assertive side of me that you just mentioned…"

"Yes…it's one of your best sides, if I may offer the compliment."

She didn't laugh or even crack a smile, for that matter. What he could see of her expression in the dim light of the bedroom looked solemn and serious.

"Yeah, well, I hate to tell you this, but that's not me."

Huh? He didn't understand where she was going with this. At least he had good sense to keep his mouth shut while she expounded, because his attempts at humor were missing the mark.

"What I mean," she finally said, "is that's not usually how I am. Or I don't know, maybe it is given the fact that it was my first time making love. The reason I was so *sexually aggressive,* as you put it, is because I was out of my mind with fear that night. I was afraid of the storm, and most of all, I was afraid I was going to die a virgin."

He was quiet. Mainly because he had no idea what to say or how to respond. For a long moment, he felt as if he were paralyzed.

That earlier well-placed kick-in-the-gut feeling that had messed with his head for a bit had returned. Only this time, it was more like someone had taken a ramrod and run it right through his center.

"I wish you would say something." Her voice was hoarse and throaty. "It wasn't easy telling you that the *last* time was actually my *first* time... Are you okay?"

* * *

There was no other way to describe Tanner's demeanor in the week since she'd told him her secret other than to call him distant and…well, just plain odd. When she asked, he kept telling her he was okay; he was still sleeping in her bed…or *his* bed, actually. The point being that they were still sharing the bed in the master suite, even if they hadn't made love since *that night*.

This was another *that night*.

Now they had two in their repertoire. Two for two. If you were able to keep score in the bedroom, it couldn't be a good thing.

He was polite, but preoccupied. And when she tried to talk to him about it, he always managed to come up with a convenient excuse: he was tired or there was an issue at work. It was always something.

This bed that they shared was getting to be a cold, lonely place.

Tanner had been working awfully hard. That's why she was glad when he'd agreed to go to the annual Red Rock Spring Fling. He might be able to run away from his fears by hiding at work, but there was no escaping Red Rock's annual festival. Jordana's sisters had been telling her how much fun it was and she was eager to experience it for herself.

Maybe a night out, away from the everyday grind, would pull them out of their funk.

They made small talk on the ride from the house to the fairgrounds. She talked about the phone calls she'd been getting from her staff at Fortune South and how nice it felt to still be needed.

"In fact, I think I'm going to talk to my father about telecommuting. If it works for me to give advice over the phone, then there is no reason I couldn't work at least part-time." Over the past week, she'd painted the room that used to be Tanner's office, put up a border with teddy bears and rocking horses. The nursery was starting to take shape.

She'd also planted the pink rosebush he'd brought home that night when everything had sprung from bad, to temporary Nirvana and then had plummeted to the depths of despair.

But the one thing that had become crystal clear since she and Tanner had taken their most recent wrong turn was that she needed more to occupy her time. At least until the baby arrived.

Tanner had only grunted when she told him of her plan to talk to her father. His unresponsive-

NANCY ROBARDS THOMPSON 203

ness set her on edge, and they needed to maintain a picture that everything was fine—at least for the time being. So Jordana decided it would be best to stay silent for the rest of the ride so that she could collect her thoughts and put on a good front.

But despite how she tried to gather herself, she couldn't escape the nagging fact that remained: she wasn't the *bold-stroke, handwriting on the wall* kind of girl that Tanner had pegged her for in the beginning, and it was a problem because she never would be that kind of woman—at least not when it came to matters of the heart.

If marriage was such a great thing, then why the hell did it make Tanner feel so bad? He suspected a big part of the reason he felt so paralyzed might be because he was making Jordana feel bad. He recognized this, but he couldn't seem to fix the situation. It was nothing specific he was doing on purpose—like saying cruel things. It was just that he needed a little space lately to process things.

Something stirred deep inside of him and a niggling feeling urged him to reach out to her— maybe just for today he could try a little compassion…to whatever end that would take them. So, when he walked around the car to open Jordana's door, he grabbed her hand as they walked toward the fairground entrance. It was a simple gesture, really, but he was surprised when she didn't pull away. She just simply held his hand.

"Where are we supposed to meet everyone?" he asked.

"Wendy said they were reserving some tables in the pavilion area. I'll call her, she can direct us in."

In the distance Tanner could see the blinking, colored lights of the rides and the midway. He'd never really been a big fan of fairs and events like this, but according to Jordana, the Spring Fling was a Fortune and Mendoza family tradition, and tonight, roll would be taken.

All the Fortunes and Mendozas would be there. Even though he wasn't very keen on going, since he'd married a Fortune, he knew he didn't really have a choice. It was times like this when he wondered what he'd gotten himself into by marrying into such a tight-knit—some might even say *controlling*—family.

"When we get inside past the ticket booth, Wendy said to follow the midway to the end and take a right. That will bring us to the pavilion."

Tanner paid for their tickets and once inside, he let Jordana lead the way. He recognized their party by its volume of people before he'd been able to pick out individuals. Jordana was all smiles, greeting her sisters and her cousins. From the looks of her, Tanner guessed no one would know they were having a hard time adjusting to marriage. In fact, by all outward standards, it appeared as if Jordana had adjusted well to married life and was now in the midst of living her very own *happily ever after.*

A pang of guilt washed over him. What was wrong with him? Ever since he'd discovered the truth about their first night together, it was as if something inside him had snapped. He hated the feeling of vulnerability that tended to render him helpless. Was that what love was supposed to be about? If so, no wonder common sense had stopped him before he'd fallen…well, until now, at least.

What scared him the most about his situation was putting his happiness, his emotional well-being in someone else's hands. When it came to that, it was as if there was an automatic kill switch inside him that shut down.

Actually, what *really* scared him the most was maybe this was what happened to his father—this same kind of raw, ripped-open feeling of being stuck in emotional purgatory—and maybe that's why he left.

He couldn't take feeling so open and vulnerable so he left first, before the situation could snowball and bury him alive.

As they made their way inside, Tanner noticed that the Fortunes were well represented—and this was only a small representation of the entire family, which was big enough to build its own army. Flint and Jessie were there with their brood of kids; Cooper and Kelsey were there with baby Anthony in tow; Jeremy and Kirsten were there; and, of course, the patriarch William Fortune and his grand dame, Lily. The Mendozas were represented, as well. Marcos and Wendy were there with baby MaryAnne; Rafe and Melina were there; as were Miguel and father, Luis.

But it was Javier Mendoza, who seemed to be in wonderful shape after recovering from the injuries he'd sustained during the tornado, who seemed to be at the center of attention. He and his fiancée, Leah, were filling glasses with champagne—or sparkling cider, for those who didn't drink alcohol.

After Javier made sure everyone had a glass in hand, he called the crowd to attention. "I'm so glad we could all be here together tonight. The end of last year started on such a happy note when we celebrated Wendy and Marcos's marriage. Unfortunately, events turned south very fast and left a lot of us in a bad way. I don't think there is a single person here who wasn't touched in some shape or form by the tornado. But sometimes good fortune masquerades as tragedy. I may never have met the love of my life had I not ended up in her care because of the injuries I sustained during the storm."

He put an arm around Leah and pulled her close. The crowd whistled and cheered, egging him on until he planted a kiss on Leah's lips. Then the Fortunes and Mendozas nearly brought down the house with their approval.

Finally, Javier continued. "What I'm trying to say is just because a situation may look bleak or tragic, it doesn't necessarily have to be. I am living proof of the power of love. If I have learned one thing through the adversity I have faced, it is to never give up on love and never underestimate its power. Life is uncertain. So if you're lucky enough to find true love, don't let a day go by where you take it for granted, because if you do you could lose it in the blink of an eye. That is why tonight, surrounded by my family and closest friends, I want to reaffirm my love for Leah and celebrate the joyous fact that she has agreed to do me the honor of spending the rest of her life with me as my wife. Leah, I vow to be worthy of your love."

With that, Javier dipped a stunned-looking Leah into a kiss that made the first one look like a handshake.

Tanner chuckled along with the hooting and

whistling crows, but something inside him felt a little hollow…perhaps, a little guilty? It was a lucky person who was sure of not just his own feelings, but trusting that the object of his affections felt the same way, too.

He hadn't been able to fully trust many people in his life, but he suddenly knew without a shred of doubt that he could trust Jordana.

A warmth that was somehow foreign and strangely familiar coursed through Tanner. Reflexively, he turned to smile at…his wife, but she wasn't there.

Sometime during the course of Javier's speech, she'd moved from Tanner's side. She'd slipped away.

He glanced around, searching the pavilion for Jordana, but he couldn't find her. He had a sinking feeling she hadn't simply slipped out to buy a Spring Fling funnel cake.

Was she gone? Something shifted inside him—a near panic that turned his blood to ice.

He wouldn't blame her if she'd left. He hadn't been very easy to live with recently. He glanced at Javier and Leah, so obviously in love. A relationship like that didn't come along every day.

If he would just let himself, he could share that same closeness with Jordana. God knew she'd tried. She'd been as patient with him as a saint, but he'd acted like a jackass.

What the hell was wrong with him? He was married to the most wonderful, giving woman in the world, yet he couldn't seem to get his own emotional act together. A voice of reason he didn't recognize that seemed to come from a place deep inside of him that he'd never known existed scolded him and told him if he didn't get himself together he was going to lose the one woman in the world he could ever love.

He started to set down his champagne glass, but Luis Mendoza raised his own to toast his son's love. Scanning the tent for any possible trace of Jordana, Tanner edged his way toward the exit as Luis saluted his son and future daughter-in-law. "It is evident that my son Javier's remarkable transformation is not just physical," said Luis. "It's simply amazing what the power of love can do for a person. So, tonight, please join me in raising a glass to Javier and Leah. May their love be blessed with many children and an eternity of happiness that they can only know with each other."

As Tanner reached the tent's exit, he hoped and prayed that he wasn't too late to save his own marriage.

Chapter Thirteen

Jordana hated to run away from such a romantic declaration, but if she'd stayed, her tears would've done more harm than her presence would've done good.

Javier's words had opened a place in Jordana that she knew she'd been ignoring for far too long. It was time to stop kidding herself. Tanner Redmond did not love her. He didn't even remotely like anything about who she was or what she represented.

He was a guy who liked bold, sexy and forward, when she was timid, two steps removed from virginity and a little prudish when it came to sharing her body. Well, maybe not prudish, just conservative. But Tanner made her feel prudish and that was no way to spend the rest of her life. As she was standing under the pavilion listening to Javier, all she could think was, *Yes, this is the way love is supposed to be.* It didn't have to be twisted and painful. Love should be the natural merging of two souls. It should be so strong that even tornado-force winds can't tear it apart.

Javier and Leah were the picture of everything that was right with love. She and Tanner were an example of a great big don't.

And to think she really had believed she could love him. Well, she did love him. That was the pathetic part. He didn't love her back. He may have been willing to stay in a relationship that was more business arrangement than it was affair of the heart, but just as Javier had pointed out, life was too short.

That's when she'd carefully worked her way to the back of the pavilion so that she could slip out unnoticed before the deluge of tears started flowing.

Unsure of what she would do once she got out into the Spring Fling crowds, her interim plan had been to find a bathroom and stay until she'd gotten control of her emotions.

But as luck would have it, she'd run almost head-on into a woman named Tracy, whom she'd met at the Stocking Stitch. Tracy was leaving and Jordana had asked if she would give her a ride home. Seeing a viable escape, Jordana managed to dam up her tears, giving Tracy the excuse that she wasn't feeling well and had lost Tanner in the crowd.

"Would you like me to help you find him? He's sure to be worried."

"Oh, no, thank you, that could take forever, and I know you're on your way out. So, if you don't mind, I'd really just like to go home and lie down."

The excuse sounded flimsy even to her own ears. What kind of man would lose his pregnant wife at a carnival? And what kind of wife would simply leave, letting her husband wonder where she was?

Jordana and Tanner. That's who.

She could tell that Tracy wasn't quite buying the flimsy pretext, but she was too polite to ask too many questions. They rode to the ranch in silence; Jordana closed her eyes most of the way, pretending to nurse whatever it was that was ailing her.

When Tracy pulled up in front of the house to

drop off Jordana, she said, "Are you sure you're okay? Do you want me to wait with you while you call a doctor? Or I'd be happy to go back to the Spring Fling and look for your husband. Does he have a cell phone? We could try calling him." Tracy's eyes brightened as if her suggestion was the long-lost answer they'd simply overlooked.

"No, thank you, really, I'll be fine if I can just get in and lie down."

Lie! Lie! Lie! her mind screamed. But she silently justified the untruth in the name of self-preservation.

It didn't take too much more convincing before Tracy was driving away. Jordana watched the taillights of her car grow smaller with a mixture of regret and relief. She was a nice person. If circumstances had been different, Jordana might even have come to call her a friend. But circumstances dictated that Jordana go inside and pack and leave on the first flight out of here bound for Atlanta.

This was the reason she had insisted on the escape clause. Now, sadly, she would exercise it.

"Excuse me, are you Jordana's husband?"

The petite woman caught Tanner by surprise. He didn't recognize her, but he wanted to hug her when he heard her utter his wife's name.

"Yes, I am," he said.

"I know you don't know me, but I'm Tracy Monroe, a friend of Jordana's. I came back to the festival to let you know that she wasn't feeling well and I gave her a ride home. I don't mean to tell you what you should do, but it might be a good idea if you went home and checked on her. She seemed pretty distraught."

The look of judgment in Tracy's eyes may have been real or perceived. Either way, Tanner felt like a schmuck for being at this damn Spring Fling festival as his wife was hitching a ride home from someone else. Why hadn't she told him she wanted to go?

"Thank you, Tracy. I'll leave now."

With a sick feeling growing in the pit of his stomach, Tanner beelined for the parking lot and floored the Tahoe most of the way home.

"Jordana?" He called her name as soon as he burst through the front doors. "Jordana, are you okay?"

She didn't answer him.

The first place he looked was in the master bedroom. And that's exactly where he found her. She was in the middle of packing her clothes and didn't even look up when he entered the room.

"Jordana, what are you doing?" He walked

around in front of her so she was forced to look at him. "Where are you going?" he pleaded.

"Home, Tanner. I'm going home."

He tried to put his hand on her shoulder, but she jerked away. "This is your home. Here with me."

She didn't say a word, but the look she shot him spoke volumes. Then she just shook her head and resumed folding her clothes and placing them into her suitcase.

"I know this might be too little too late, but I realized a lot tonight. The very least of which is I don't know how I will live without you."

She kept about her chore and didn't look at him.

"I know I've been acting like a total horse's ass lately and I'm sorry, I wish more than anything I could have a do-over or at least a chance to make it up to you."

From the stoic look on her face, he might as well have been repeating the word *blah blah blah blah*. That's when the very real horror hit him. He was about to lose the only woman he'd ever loved. Probably the only woman he would ever be able to love.

"Please listen to me." He put both hands on her shoulders and gently turned her around to face him. He was surprised that she let him do it.

Somehow he knew he had one shot, and he'd better make it good.

"So you know how I was your first lover?" Her eyebrow shot up in a fashion that seemed to say, *Really?* You're going to go *there?* Idiot.

"Well, you are my first *love*. Jordana, I have never been in love before and I know I've messed up things terribly, but I can't lose you. I love you."

The incredulous look vanished from her face. In its place was a look of…awe. She opened her mouth as if to say something, but no words came out. She closed her mouth and bit her bottom lip in a gesture that had become so familiar to him… so *her*…that it made him ache with longing.

Then she closed her eyes, but tears escaped, anyway.

"Tanner, I can't stay in a marriage that isn't real. Tonight, did you see Javier and Leah? Did you hear what he said and see the way he looked at her? That's love. This separate-bedroom, worlds-apart arrangement even when we are in the same bed isn't going to work. I will go along with whatever custody agreement we can fairly draw up, but living this way is just too hard."

No. He wouldn't let her go. He couldn't.

"Please don't go. Because I love you and I don't

know what I will do if I lose you. Please give me a chance to make it up to you."

She was quiet, but at least she wasn't turning away from him. Her stillness encouraged him to continue.

"I want you to be my wife for the long haul, and I will do whatever it takes to prove that to you. I've never done this before. So, I need you to help me. All I know is that you've gotten under my skin, and I guess it scared me when I felt a little out of control of the situation.

"For all my experience, I've never felt like this before and it scared me. Like a typical man, I needed time to work through those feelings and what it really means to give myself to another person. I just hope I'm not too late."

Jordana sat down on the edge of the bed.

"I don't want to leave, Tanner. I want to make a life with you and the baby more than I've ever wanted anything. But I can't take this back-and-forth business. I can't live in a world where I'm the Madonna mother of your child, but you need a wild woman in the bedroom. I'm not either of those. I'm certainly not perfect, but I'm not the woman who seduced you the night of the storm, either. I guess I'm somewhere in between. And I need to know that that's enough for you."

A rush of relief flooded through him, and he hoped he wasn't jumping to the conclusion he wanted to see—he seemed to be doing a lot of that lately and it had landed him in a big mess.

"You are just perfect for me. If I have to spend the rest of my life proving that to you, that will be my life's work."

"What about the flight school? You would let that take a backseat to pursuing me?"

The humor had returned to her voice. And she was smiling again. Tanner drew in a shaky deep breath.

"I will move heaven and earth and all of my students if that's what it takes to prove my love to you."

Then she was in his arms.

"This is the best way you can prove your love to me. Just hold on to me and never let me go. Deal?"

He sealed the deal with a kiss delivered to rock her world.

"Mrs. Redmond, you have yourself a deal."

* * * * *

HEART & HOME

Heartwarming romances where love can
happen right when you least expect it.

◆ Harlequin®
SPECIAL EDITION®

COMING NEXT MONTH
AVAILABLE MAY 29, 2012

#2191 FORTUNE'S PERFECT MATCH
The Fortunes of Texas: Whirlwind Romance
Allison Leigh

#2192 ONCE UPON A MATCHMAKER
Matchmaking Mamas
Marie Ferrarella

#2193 THE RANCHER'S HIRED FIANCÉE
Brighton Valley Babies
Judy Duarte

#2194 THE CAMDEN COWBOY
Northbridge Nuptials
Victoria Pade

#2195 AN OFFICER, A BABY AND A BRIDE
The Foster Brothers
Tracy Madison

#2196 NO ORDINARY JOE
Michelle Celmer

You can find more information on upcoming Harlequin® titles,
free excerpts and more at www.HarlequinInsideRomance.com.

HSECNM0512

REQUEST YOUR FREE BOOKS!
2 FREE NOVELS PLUS 2 FREE GIFTS!

♦ Harlequin®

SPECIAL EDITION
Life, Love & Family

YES! Please send me 2 FREE Harlequin® Special Edition novels and my 2 FREE gifts (gifts are worth about $10). After receiving them, if I don't wish to receive any more books, I can return the shipping statement marked "cancel." If I don't cancel, I will receive 6 brand-new novels every month and be billed just $4.49 per book in the U.S. or $5.24 per book in Canada. That's a saving of at least 14% off the cover price! It's quite a bargain! Shipping and handling is just 50¢ per book in the U.S. and 75¢ per book in Canada.* I understand that accepting the 2 free books and gifts places me under no obligation to buy anything. I can always return a shipment and cancel at any time. Even if I never buy another book, the two free books and gifts are mine to keep forever.

235/335 HDN FEGF

Name	(PLEASE PRINT)	

Address		Apt. #

City	State/Prov.	Zip/Postal Code

Signature (if under 18, a parent or guardian must sign)

Mail to the **Reader Service:**
IN U.S.A.: P.O. Box 1867, Buffalo, NY 14240-1867
IN CANADA: P.O. Box 609, Fort Erie, Ontario L2A 5X3

Not valid for current subscribers to Harlequin Special Edition books.

Want to try two free books from another line?
Call 1-800-873-8635 or visit www.ReaderService.com.

* Terms and prices subject to change without notice. Prices do not include applicable taxes. Sales tax applicable in N.Y. Canadian residents will be charged applicable taxes. Offer not valid in Quebec. This offer is limited to one order per household. All orders subject to credit approval. Credit or debit balances in a customer's account(s) may be offset by any other outstanding balance owed by or to the customer. Please allow 4 to 6 weeks for delivery. Offer available while quantities last.

Your Privacy—The Reader Service is committed to protecting your privacy. Our Privacy Policy is available online at www.ReaderService.com or upon request from the Reader Service.

We make a portion of our mailing list available to reputable third parties that offer products we believe may interest you. If you prefer that we not exchange your name with third parties, or if you wish to clarify or modify your communication preferences, please visit us at www.ReaderService.com/consumerschoice or write to us at Reader Service Preference Service, P.O. Box 9062, Buffalo, NY 14269. Include your complete name and address.

HSE11B

SPECIAL EDITION

Life, Love and Family

USA TODAY bestselling author

Marie Ferrarella

enchants readers in

ONCE UPON A MATCHMAKER

Micah Muldare's aunt is worried that her nephew is going to wind up alone in his old age…but this matchmaking mama has just the thing! When Micah finds himself accused of theft, defense lawyer Tracy Ryan agrees to help him as a favor to his aunt, but soon finds herself drawn to more than just his case. Will Micah open up his heart and realize Tracy is his match?

Available June 2012

Saddle up with Harlequin® series books this summer and find a cowboy for every mood!

Available wherever books are sold.

HSE65674

A grim discovery is about to change everything for Detective Layne Sullivan—including how she interacts with her boss!

Read on for an exciting excerpt of the upcoming book UNRAVELING THE PAST by Beth Andrews....

SOMETHING WAS UP—otherwise why would Chief Ross Taylor summon her back out? As Detective Layne Sullivan walked over, she grudgingly admitted he was doing well. But that didn't change the fact that the Chief position should have been hers.

Taylor turned as she approached. "Detective Sullivan, we have a situation."

"What's the problem?"

He aimed his flashlight at the ground. The beam illuminated a dirt-encrusted skull.

"Definitely a problem." And not something she'd expected. Not here. "How'd you see it?"

"Jess stumbled upon it looking for her phone."

Layne looked to where his niece huddled on a log. "I'll contact the forensics lab."

"Already have a team on the way. I've also called in units to search for the rest of the remains."

So he'd started the ball rolling. Then, she'd assume command while he took Jess home. "I have this under control."

Though it was late, he was clean shaven and neat, his flat stomach a testament to his refusal to indulge in doughnuts. His dark blond hair was clipped at the sides, the top long enough to curl.

The female part of Layne admitted he was attractive.

The cop in her resented the hell out of him for it.

"You get a lot of missing-persons cases here?" he asked.

"People don't go missing from Mystic Point." Although plenty of them left. "But we have our share of crime."

"I'll take the lead on this one."

Bad enough he'd come to *her* town and taken the position she was meant to have, now he wanted to mess with *how* she did her job? "Why? I'm the only detective on third shift and your second in command."

"Careful, Detective, or you might overstep."

But she'd never played it safe.

"I don't think it's overstepping to clear the air. You have something against me?"

"I assign cases based on experience and expertise. You don't have to like how I do that, but if you need to question every decision, perhaps you'd be happier somewhere else."

"Are you threatening my job?"

He moved so close she could feel the warmth from his body. "I'm not threatening anything." His breath caressed her cheek. "I'm giving you the choice of what happens next."

What will Layne choose? Find out in
UNRAVELING THE PAST by Beth Andrews,
available June 2012 from Harlequin® Superromance®.

And be sure to look for the other two books
in Beth's THE TRUTH ABOUT THE SULLIVANS series
available in August and October 2012.

Copyright © 2012 by Beth Burgoon

HSREXP0612

Harlequin Romance

A touching new duet from fan-favorite author

SUSAN MEIER

First Time DADS!

When millionaire CEO Max Montgomery spots
Kate Hunter-Montgomery—the wife he's never forgotten—
back in town with a daughter who looks just like him, he's
determined to win her back. But can this savvy business tycoon
convince Kate to trust him a second time with her heart?

Find out this June in

THE TYCOON'S SECRET DAUGHTER

And look for book 2 coming this August!

NANNY FOR THE MILLIONAIRE'S TWINS

Saddle up with Harlequin® series books this summer
and find a cowboy for every mood!

www.Harlequin.com

HRI7811